# Praise for Ken Kalfus and

# *THIRST*

"The stories in *THIRST* come at Ken Kalfus' readers from left of center, from surprising places not located on the banks of the mainstream. . . . The fable 'Invisible Malls' is a delicious fantasy. . . ."

—*The New York Times Book Review*

"Playful, moving short stories about travel, childhood, and loss, from a writer who does almost everything well."
—*Paper* magazine

"Kalfus is one of those rare writers whose travels haven't colored his prose with cosmopolitan cynicism. . . . He reminds us that sometimes the really significant truths are those found closest to home."

—*The Village Voice*

"Ken Kalfus is a writer with the rare, hermetic gift of traveling so effortlessly between the realm of experience and the realm of spirit and imagination that the boundary between them appears seamless. His stories are genuinely magical, that is, the transformations they work are real, not illusions. *THIRST* is a collection steeped in wonder."

—Stuart Dybek

"The quality that gives a short story legs, the one that makes it memorable long after it was read, is naked imagination. And it is Kalfus' imagination—so unique yet so universally applicable—that lifts the stories above the ordinary. . . . He also has a very convincing ability to get inside the minds of fictitious others of very different backgrounds. . . ."

—Minneapolis *Star-Tribune*

"At once fantastic, absurd, and satirical, *THIRST* is a perverse commentary on and comical prediction of American culture. . . . The fourteen stories in this collection are stylistically wide-ranging, buoyed by witty narrators, diverse protagonists, and enticing settings: the locales range from New York to Paris, from a jungle in Southeast Asia to suburban Long Island. They engage the reader's attention and imagination from start to finish. . . ."

—*Booklist*

"Kalfus veers between whimsical postmodern playfulness and a darker realism in the fourteen stories of his skilled, versatile first collection. . . . Ambitious and daring, with smart, fluid prose and an abundance of surprises."

—*Publishers Weekly*

# THIRST

## Ken Kalfus

WASHINGTON SQUARE PRESS
PUBLISHED BY POCKET BOOKS

New York  London  Toronto  Sydney  Tokyo  Singapore

Versions of these stories first appeared in the following publications:

"Notice," Bouquet," "Invisible Malls," and "A Line Is a Series of Points"
in the *North American Review;* "Thirst," "The Joy and Melancholy Baseball Trivia Quiz," and "No Grace on the Road" in the *Sonora Review;*
"Cats in Space" in the *Inquirer Magazine;* "The Republic of St. Mark,
1849" in the *Village Voice Literary Supplement;* "Night and Day You Are
the One" in *Boulevard;* "Among the Bulgarians" in the *Literary Review;*
"Suit" in the *Penn Review;* "The Weather in New York" in *Boca Raton.*

 A Washington Square Press Publication of
POCKET BOOKS, a division of Simon & Schuster Inc.
1230 Avenue of the Americas, New York, NY 10020

Copyright © 1998 by Ken Kalfus

Published by arrangement with Milkweed Editions

ISBN: 0-671-03482-0

First Washington Square Press trade paperback printing September 1999

10  9  8  7  6  5  4  3  2

WASHINGTON SQUARE PRESS and colophon are
registered trademarks of Simon & Schuster Inc.

Cover design by Brigid Pearson
Front cover photo by Steve McAfee/The Stock Illustration Source

Printed in the U.S.A.

# For Inga

*Sullivan Street, Rue de la Sorbonne, Cromwellsfort Road,*
*Lennox Street, East Fourth Street, Main Street, Route 202,*
*West Seventh Street, Kater Street, Ulica Gospodar Jevremova,*
*Ulica Vojislava Vukovica, West Rittenhouse Square,*
*Kutuzovsky Prospekt*

# Thirst

". . . but it is a melancholy of mine own,
compounded of many simples, extracted from many
objects, and indeed the sundry contemplation of my
travels, in which my often rumination wraps me in a
most humorous sadness."

*As You Like It*
Act IV, Scene I

# THIRST

# Notice

such requests in a favorable light as, the above sentence notwithstanding, he seeks to have this paragraph communicated in all languages and by all technologies, not for personal or proprietary reasons, but to bring another facet of the whole that exists to general awareness. Just drop me a note. My e-mail address is 72754.2514@compuserve.com. Except in the case of obvious satirical intent (an exception that applies to this entire paragraph, which resembles the device that provides copyright protection but is without that protection itself), all the characters in this paragraph are fictitious, and any resemblance to actual persons, living or dead, including the author, is purely coincidental, or at least unpredictable. Between what we describe and the truth lies a poorly marked border, and in a writer's desperate wanderings he will occasionally cross it and then, unawares, meander back (I'm not quite satisfied with the above description of ditto ink. There are other details: the paper soaked up the blue, plumping and softening the letters, as if it too were intoxicated by the ink; this lightened the letters' color, slightly empurpling them, a transformation that defied simile until I witnessed the rush of twilight one summer morning a few years later; I never saw the ditto machine but imagined it as a hand-powered, gracefully constructed device of a few large gears and levers; the sight of thirty adolescents pressing inky sheets of paper against their faces as if, I imagine now, engaged in some cultish ceremony never seemed remarkable; a girl whom I had known since kindergarten, traveling with her up through our schools' grades and departmentalized classes on frequently intersecting paths without ever quite having a conversation, might pull the paper away with a sigh of such explosiveness that I would be momentarily excited and a little in love, and then frightened, reminded of her inscrutability; in our suburban, earnestly innocent school we dared fate with jokes about needing our narcotic "fix" of the ink; crumbling pages of tests and assignments from October and November, months that seemed in April and May like a much earlier, more promising, forever lost part of childhood, after a couple of seasons at the bottom of my locker bore a faded, uninspiring scent, which was mostly a function of memory. The memory still resists full description. After such failure, of what use is a copyright?). This paragraph contains the complete text of the hardcover edition. NOT ONE WORD HAS BEEN OMITTED.

# Le Jardin de la Sexualité

# Bouquet

The young au pair had grown up only twenty minutes from Grafton Street, in the pastel-colored clapboard suburb of Finglas, and she had expected Paris to be somewhat like Dublin, if bigger. But automobiles here careened down narrow streets, a subtle and capricious grammar tied the language in knots, men and women in flowing desert robes passed her as she walked the children home from school, and everywhere, on everyone's minds, on the tips of their tongues, like a secret they could not keep, there was sex. On the way to the museum with Marie and Melanie one afternoon, Nula entered a metro station in which every billboard carried the same advertisement for a line of lingerie. The adverts were huge, reaching from floor to ceiling, and were composed entirely of a close-up photograph of two breasts gently cupped by a white lace bra. The image was repeated on nearly every inch of wall space in the station, even alongside the system map, all the way down the stairs, and then on every platform. As the train pulled from the station, the breasts flickered in Nula's eyes.

The girls, ages ten and eight, didn't miss any of it. No, they wouldn't. They stared at the advertisements and, once aboard the train, launched into a discussion about a schoolmate who had begun wearing a brassiere.

"She stuffs it with tissue paper!" cried Melanie, the eight-year-old.

The two of them fell against each other, giggling. The other passengers looked away.

Marie and Melanie knew the au pair's discomfort; this was their revenge. They hated museums. They would have preferred to spend their Wednesday afternoons, when school was let out early, in the Luxembourg Gardens children's park or at Trocadero, where they would watch helmeted youths, some just a little older than Marie, glide and spin on skateboards down the Palais de Chaillot's long driveways. Nula had taken them there once but, burdened by the knowledge that the French school authorities had thoughtfully set aside the half day for educational excursions, she now insisted on searching the newspapers for exhibitions, matinees, and recitals.

It was their first visit to this museum, a majestic block of carved stone, not like those joke structures, all glass and plumbing fixtures, that had been thrown up around the city in the last few decades. Dedicated to the diffusion of scientific knowledge, it sailed through the neatly tended, grassy square like a battleship trimmed with granite weaponry and other appurtenances: a tower, a clock, a gallery of togaed figures perched between decks. Nula swept up the steps with the girls, past a scattering of men sunning themselves at the institution's prow. Some of them squatted and spat seeds. An elder passed, dangling a single watch for sale from a rough, misshapen hand. Teeth flashed at an unkind remark.

A young man lounged by the museum door, wearing a brown leather jacket and a rakishly askew, oversized plaid cap. He stared at each woman passerby, regardless of her age or appearance, fishing for her eye, and mechanically moved on to the next one after she was gone. It was the cap that caught Nula's attention: its vulgarity amplified his projection of self-confidence. He thought he was good-looking enough to wear anything. Nula glanced at the youth for only a moment, but the moment was too long, for he smiled at her and knew that she saw him smile.

She looked away, but before she and the girls could enter the building he had reached them. "Good day," he said. His politeness just accented the tiny leer that began around his eyes and turned up the little parabolas of skin at the ends of his mouth.

"Excuse us," she replied in French, passing the children around him.

"English?" he guessed.

"No," she said, and was in the door. Melanie started to look back at the youth, but the au pair seized her and thrust her into the queue at the ticket counter.

When it was time for their baths, the girls would dodge her, running through the flat stark naked, hiding underneath the dining-room table, and once even dashing out onto the terrace to display themselves to the whole of Passy. They were hardly better behaved in their parents' company. The other night after dinner, when Nula came in from the kitchen with the coffee, she found that Marie had stuck two cups under her shirt and was playing the vamp with Melanie, who examined her sister's chest with mock lust. But Madame Reynourd had only suppressed a laugh and lightly scolded them: *"Dégoûtant!"*

Monsieur and Madame Reynourd were easy-going people, if a bit disorganized. They shambled through their flat either half dressed or half undressed—Nula could never be sure in which direction their disarray was heading; they left large sums of cash lying about; they could never remember what plans had been agreed for the children that day. Already in their forties and each a stone overweight, they were nevertheless enveloped in a kind of ripe, luxuriant youthfulness. Paul played rugby on Sundays and came home soaked in sweat. Elizabeth wore her blouses virtually unbuttoned. She flirted with the husbands of friends and, accompanying Nula to the butcher and baker, even with the young shop assistants, on the au pair's behalf. Nula nearly cowered behind her. At night in her room several stories above their flat, she lay awake and, against the current of intention, her thoughts drifted to the couple below and their seething sexual restlessness.

The girls' inability to concentrate descended from their parents like a congenital stain. Here on the second floor of the museum, within a glass case, a tree bloomed with stuffed tropical birds outlandishly feathered and preserved so close to the edge of life that Nula could, or thought she should, almost hear them singing, but what drew Marie's attention was the device that recorded on a rolling scroll the humidity behind the glass. Nula shooed her away from it. The two girls began to jog

toward an exhibit describing the construction of the
Eiffel Tower and then—in a moment of insight—realized
that the surface friction of the hall's polished marble
floors was less than the forward momentum of a little
girl in new penny-loafers. They slid the rest of the way.

"Marie! Melanie! Stop!" Nula hissed. The young man
(an Algerian? a Libyan?) approached, grinning. He had
followed them into the museum and had been shad-
owing them through it. He had lurked near her in the
dark of the astronomy exhibit, his bared teeth purple in
the ultraviolet light. In the metallurgy hall, he had
stared intently as she read to Marie the explanation of
how an iron forge worked.

"Come here," she now called to the children, but,
embarrassed in his presence, she called too softly for
them to hear, or at least softly enough for them to pretend not to hear.

"Well, you are a American?" the Algerian confidently
asked in uncertain English. "You are a student maybe.
I am a student. Do you know Vincennes?"

"No." Her education had gone no further than her
secondary school leaving certificate.

"My degree is almost finished," he said. "I am two
years at Jussieu, and now I am at Vincennes, at the
Department of Sexology."

Nula didn't reply. She looked past him, at the children, who ignored her.

"Do you know the sexology field? Very fascinating
field. We are the most foremost department in Europe
and America. We include the study of anatomy, anthro-
pology, mass culture, economy, philosophy, human

relations. The whole gamut, as it were. Every academic discipline must include a contemplation of human sex, don't you agree?"

Marie and Melanie, having exhausted their interest in nineteenth-century engineering, took another run and, squealing, slid out of the hall. Nula shook her head at the Algerian and took off after them at a brisk trot, mentally compiling a list of punishments, through one coolly lit hall after another, past the minerals exhibit and the insects and through the computer room, whose collection of computing instruments began with a Chinese abacus and ended with a model of a large punched card *ordinateur* dating from the Fourth Republic. Every time she thought she had lost their trail, she heard the girls giggle and shriek, and they'd skitter through the door at the far end of the room.

But then, when she was sure they had gone as far as they could into the dim recesses of the building, Nula found herself in a large, bright, completely modern hall, with the girls standing right there before her, as quiet and attentive as a pair of dolls. The au pair's face was moist. She could feel the wetness above her lips.

"Now you'll catch it," she said in English. She hunkered and roughly fastened a few buttons on Melanie's blue school uniform that had come undone. "Mama will hear of this, I promise you. No television tonight. And don't ask me to buy you cakes on the way home. You've been very, very naughty."

But the girls weren't listening. Nula turned, looked up at the object of their attention, and gasped. The opposite wall contained a floor-to-ceiling backlit color transparency of a man and woman, standing shoulder to shoulder, completely naked. Their arms were at their sides, their private parts exposed. The couple were perched on a diving board and behind them were a range of forested hills and a rich blue sky. Their smiles were placid, as if they noticed neither each other nor the camera. Nula fell silent. The man's penis seemed small in relation to the rest of him; the mossy equilateral between the woman's legs was exceptionally black. Then Marie said something—Nula didn't hear what—to Melanie, and they both giggled.

"Oh, this is *biology,*" Nula said, her mouth dry. "Come, let's look at the rocket ships."

"We want to stay," Marie told her.

"We can't."

"Why not?"

"It's boring," Nula said.

Marie and Melanie remained where they were. Nula took a few steps toward the exit, and the girls, less tentatively, went in the other direction.

The entire hall was devoted to reproduction and sexuality. A film projection demonstrated amoebas splitting. A DNA spiral stairway climbed to the ceiling. Next to it, a plastic model the size of a school bus showed the pistil and stamens of an archetypical flower, accompanied by a softly buzzing mechanical bee suspended from wires. One display diagrammed the courtship dance of two hummingbirds; another the egg-laying strategies of frogs; a third showed two elephants mating.

Side by side were similar exhibits explaining human reproduction, as if men and women were no more than rutting animals (they're no *less*, Elizabeth would say). Across from the elephants was a diagram of the developing human fetus, along with a picture of the completely naked mother, her breasts splayed, her belly distended, at the corresponding stages of pregnancy. An actual fetus floated in an amber liquid in a display case below the diagram. Nula's two charges stood by it, making little trilling sounds of awe. Nula herself stared for a moment, shivered, and then remembered the girls.

"Don't you want to see the butterflies?"

But they had already moved on to the next exhibit, drawings of the human male and female at progressive ages, including labeled diagrams of their genitals. And, squatting by them, talking quickly and in earnest, was the Algerian! The tawny skin between the top of his jeans and the bottom of his shirt shone like the skin of a piece of fruit. Marie and Melanie listened attentively.

"Monsieur!" Nula cried. The girls snickered. "What are you doing? What do you want?"

He stood and offered her a warm smile as she approached. "My little friends were asking of me some few questions."

"Their questions are not for you to answer," she said. "Leave it to their mother."

"Madame—" he began, allowing a question mark to bob in the pause.

But Nula said, "I'm not their mother," turned to the children, and briskly told them, "Let's go."

Melanie danced away from under her arm. She joined her sister to stare into the next display case, their faces pressed against it. The idea of the dirt squeezing into the pores of the girls' skin disgusted Nula. She glanced inside the case. It contained a variety of devices, accompanied by a text and diagrams that described their uses. She didn't recognize a single one.

"Look, here's a playground!" she said desperately, glimpsing a patch of green outside an open door around the corner. "Don't you want to play?"

The two girls ignored her. Nula cooed, pleaded, and demanded—and finally bribed them outside with the promise of a bag of chestnuts. They held out for ice cream, and even then had to be shoved out the door. As they left, the Algerian winked at her.

In the small park and sculpture garden adjacent to the museum, old men sitting on weathered benches gazed at the statuary; couples strolled arm and arm along the park's paths. Nula bought the girls two chocolate *esquimaux* from a vendor. "We have a half hour," she told them. "Have fun."

She might as well have told them to do the following week's homework. "Play," she said, and finally they sulked off down a tightly manicured row of rose hedges, ice cream already dripping to their fists.

Nula was glad to be free of them for the moment. She could find a bench and relax, and perhaps enjoy an ice cream herself. The park was lovely. The flowers were in bloom, the day had turned fair. She wished they had come here from the start. The girls were too young for science.

"*Canadienne?*"

She turned and glared at the Algerian standing beside her. He grinned.

"You're a terrible man to fill their ears with such filth," she told him.

"Filth?"

"The way you talk and they're so young."

"But sex is part of life."

"I won't have it," Nula said, her temper rising. "There's a proper age for everything, and a proper way of learning about this."

"What age, what way did you learn it?"

"Sexology. I don't believe there is such a thing."

"Are you a virgin?"

"Yes I am," she said.

The defiant admission made her flush. She had never told anyone this before. Yet she did not regret the confession: She enjoyed its recklessness. She had told the truth as if it didn't matter.

The Algerian merely nodded his head in a professional manner.

"Have you a boyfriend?"

"Go away."

"It is best," he said pleasantly, "that the first time be with someone who understands the necessary gentleness and is also very expert."

"The first time will be with someone I love."

The Algerian's shrug was nearly Gallic. "Why begin love with anxiety and frustration?"

"Where I come from, people look for romance. You don't study that, do you?"

"On the contrary—"

"If you don't go I'm calling the police. There's a guard over there. Are your residency papers in order?" Nula was looking directly into the Algerian's face as she said this, but she missed the moment his expression changed. He still wore a smile, but his face had hardened around it, leaving his smile not too far from a grimace. The transformation revealed that he was hardly older than she was. The ridiculous cap on his head now looked like something he had to wear because he didn't own another. The youth started to speak—a retort, a challenge, something fierce—but he interrupted himself to say, "I'm very regretful to have made a disturbance."

He abruptly turned, passed through the door into the museum, and disappeared around an exhibit devoted to venereal disease.

The au pair strolled alone through the labyrinth of hedges and abstract statuary. She was angry at herself and embarrassed by her shrillness. She wished she hadn't made the remark about the Algerian's residence permit. There were many people in Paris who didn't have the proper papers, yet had nowhere else to go. And in the end, the Algerian had been harmless, even flattering. When was the last time (she imagined Madame Reynourd asking her) a man had courted her with such persistence? Of course, she had no choice but to ask him to leave (she imagined telling Elizabeth), but (she admitted) she needn't have been unkind.

Nula turned a corner and found Marie and Melanie studying a statue, smiles of delight and discovery playing on their faces. This cheered her. No matter what ugliness and corruption there was in this world, Paris's beauty was fair compensation. She stepped beside the girls, gently running a hand through Melanie's long hair, and examined the unusual, centaurlike mass of bronze. It suddenly resolved: a man behind a woman, both on their knees, his hands firmly gripping her hips.

"It's bad!" she cried, pulling the girls away. "Bad! We're leaving *now!*"

Nula raced Marie and Melanie, momentarily silenced by her vehemence, down one lane and then another, past a dozen statues that only now were recognizable. Nearly every one showed a man and woman in some position of copulation—and those that didn't, well they were much worse. *Prière de ne pas laisser de détritus,* no littering, warned a sign along one path, and under the warning was the legend, *Musée de l'Histoire Naturelle: Jardin de la Sexualité.* "Don't look," Nula shrieked as they passed a grouping of marble figures demonstrating several forms of oral sex.

As soon as they reached the street, Nula furiously cleaned the girls' ice cream-smeared hands and faces with the premoistened towelettes she always carried in her purse.

"You're *hurting* me," Marie whined.

"Being clean doesn't hurt."

"The woman was drinking the man's pee-pee," Melanie said.

Her sister started to explain, but Nula shouted, *"Shut your mouth!"*

Marie replied with an obscenity.

Someone called from across the street. "Mademoiselle, Mademoiselle!" Nula, still on her haunches, didn't need to look up.

"Bloody hell," she muttered.

"Mademoiselle," the Algerian called again, dodging traffic. He approached, breathing hard. "Accept my apology please for such misunderstanding that I made."

He thrust a bouquet in her face.

Stunned, Nula rose and took the flowers, a clutch of white lilies, yellow peonies, tulips, and a single sunflower, wrapped in newspaper.

The Algerian said, "I too look for romance."

Nula kept her lips pressed together, maintaining her expression of annoyance.

"I want that you should see," the man added. He removed a black vinyl wallet from his jeans. In it was his *carte de séjour*, his resident permit. On the card, under his long, unpronounceable family name and his twentieth arrondissement address, was a line reserved for his profession: *étudiant*.

"I have right in Paris like you," he told her. There was less rancor in this statement than pride. Nula had come to France on the ferry from Rosslare; his journey had been much more difficult.

"So you do," she said evenly.

Marie and Melanie stared at the Algerian and then at the flowers. Marie sniffed at the bouquet. "They're nice," she mumbled, dazed by his gallantry.

"Well then. I now say farewell ladies. Farewell."

The Algerian, or perhaps he was a Libyan or even

a Tunisian, bowed and straightened, then turned on the heels of his Adidas and hurried down the street. He didn't look back before he vanished around the corner. "Men like that," Nula began to tell the girls, but she didn't complete the sentence. She really didn't know men like that at all.

By the time they reached home, by way of a crowded, overheated train, Nula, Marie, and Melanie were exhausted. Madame Reynourd met them in the flat's foyer and asked if they enjoyed the museum. Marie said it was boring, and she and her sister trudged off to their bedroom unbuttoning their school uniforms.

"And how was your afternoon?" Elizabeth asked Nula.

"Marvelous," Nula said.

It was then that Elizabeth noticed the flowers, still in Nula's hands, unwilted and fragrant despite the crush of the metro. Elizabeth raised her eyebrows in an expression of curious amusement. But Nula, surprised by her own reply, didn't wish to answer any more questions. She pushed past her, hurriedly explaining, "I must put these in some water."

Nula found a blue cut glass vase in the kitchen cabinet and ran the tap. She removed the cellotape and unfurled the newspaper. As the flowers shifted, an object fell from between their stalks and onto the tiled floor. It was a key chain, without keys, and attached to it was a small tag with a phone number written on it in a very tight, careful print, and a charm: an anatomically correct, dusky plastic phallus.

Nula put her hands to her chest and shrieked, and she was sure the shriek reached every flat in the building, and into the concierge's office, and onto the street, frightening passersby and perhaps even stopping traffic. But when Madame Reynourd came into the kitchen, it was with an unalarmed step and, when she saw what lay on the floor, it raised a soft, pleased smile.

# Thirst

In hesitant, ungrammatical English occasionally swept clean by a gust of fluency, he told her that once while traveling across the desert, he had lost his way, and then his water. He nearly died, or perhaps he did die, and Paris was heaven. If so, he had first passed through hell, on the back of a rasping, worn-out camel. He told her that his lips had become puffy and cracked, his throat burned, he could hardly breathe. He was so dehydrated he had stopped perspiring. He passed in and out of delirium: He thought that he had entered a great but waterless city. Its people lined its unshaded boulevards, their stares reproaching him for his empty canteen. He rode further into the desert, no longer recalling his direction. When he dismounted he discovered that he could barely stand. He pulled his prayer mat from his pack, laid it on the baked sand in front of the animal, and wrapped his hand with a piece of cloth from his headdress. Then he shoved his fist between the camel's jaws. As he pushed his fingers against the back of its tongue, the camel bucked and tried to bite, but he held on to the beast with all that was left of his life. Finally, throwing its long, mournful head forward and furiously stamping the ground, and with a strangled, almost human cry, the camel vomited. Henri drank the vomit off the mat.

"You're revolting," Nula said, jarred fully awake. She

had been gazing through the skylight and had lost herself in the desolate afternoon sky. She turned to him and lifted her head onto the heel of her hand.

He said, "A day later I reached a wadi."

They had met the day before at a bistro. His name was Henri, a French name, but his surname was Tatahouine. She had asked him to spell it. He was Moroccan. Nula didn't tell Madame Reynourd that she had phoned him, nor that she was going to see him, but she left his name and the name of the bistro on a note pad in a prominent position on her dresser. Just in case.

Just in case what? That she'd be abducted? Attacked? What? All week the twenty-year-old au pair had been in a peculiar state of mind, some species of happy dread. She knew she would eventually sleep with the Arab, and thereby lose that nearly abstract quality, or condition, that had seemed to have become her most tangible characteristic, but she had expected Paris to be its undoing anyway, and the waiting was worse than anything that might in fact happen. The Arab was her fate; so be it. She was not afraid. She had already proved that by leaving Ireland. And even as she was made dizzy by the thought of what she was doing, she was telling herself she would keep her head. If he wanted her, he would have to court her. She had nearly rung off when he suggested that she come directly to his flat. No, it would have to be at a bistro.

Nula arrived early and took a window table that commanded every approach to the bistro. The place she had instructed him to meet her was in the fifteenth arrondissement, prudently close to home but far enough that if this meeting turned out unpleasantly, she would not often be reminded of it. She ordered an orange mineral water. Sipping from the tall, sweaty glass, she wondered where she'd be in a few hours, how she'd feel. She tried to see into the future, but what she found was hazier than the memory of a dream: shadows and inaudible murmurs too vague to warn her if she were about to make a terrible mistake.

A warm hand touched the back of her shoulder and lightly massaged it. She twisted away, spilling some of her drink. It was Henri, coming out of the kitchen.

"Good day, is it not?" he said, grinning at the alarm he read on her face. "A fine day to fall in love, I think."

"You work here?" she said, coloring.

He took the seat opposite her without removing his faded leather jacket or his cap. "My cousins," he explained.

Another Arab, a busboy, passed by and winked. Nula glared at the youth.

"I am a student," Henri reminded her.

"Yes."

"I hope that you did not need to wait much time."

"Only a few minutes," she said, sopping up the pale little puddles of her drink with a tissue from her purse.

"No, I mean, wait much time to meet a fellow like me."

"You're a real charmer, do you know that?"

"Thank you."

Elegantly raising his index finger, he summoned a

waiter. Nula didn't understand what Henri told him. Henri then said in English, "My girlfriend would like . . ." and turned to her with a solicitous smile.

"What I have now is fine thank you," she said, though in fact there was hardly anything left to it.

Henri shrugged and grinned at the waiter but tried again when he quickly returned with an unrecognizable black liquid in a sherry glass.

"Terrack," Henri said. "May I offer you some?"

"I'm not thirsty."

"It is very tasty."

"I prefer cold drinks."

"Would you like a beer? Beers are cold. In Ireland, I know, there are many beers: Guinness, Smithwick's, Murphy's, Harp . . ." He added, "In America, the beer is very cold, so that it hurts the teeth. Budweiser. Miller."

"Have you been to America?" she asked abruptly. It came out like a challenge.

He sipped his drink, washed it around his mouth, grimaced, and wiped his face with his hand.

"Wouldn't you like a glass?"

She shook her head.

"Not even for a taste?" He again signalled the waiter.

"I won't drink it!" Nula insisted, more vehemently than she intended. "I don't want any."

Henri looked hurt. "This is what we drink in my country."

"We're not in your country."

"This is what we offer our neighbors, our family. This is how we begin friendships. It is an insult to turn down a drink."

"I'm not thirsty," she repeated. The waiter was bringing it anyway.

Henri laughed without smiling. "In my country," he said, "we are always thirsty. Do you know the rainfall amount in Morocco per year?"

He waited for an answer, even after she shook her head. Finally she said, "I don't know anything about Morocco."

"What do you think? A meter? Do you think 20 centimeters? Is that possible? It is a very small amount, you know. Paris gets fifty-six centimeters. Twenty centimeters is not much at all. So what do you think?"

"All right, twenty centimeters then."

Henri snorted and leaned over the table. "Twenty centimeters, hah! Not even half that. Not even again half. The average rainfall, if you add the coast of the Atlantic and the north—there is more rain there than in the south—is less than a centimeter for the entire year. In the southern desert, nothing grows, except in the wadis, and there the grass is just clumps of weeds. And do you know that every year the desert is bigger than the year before? Yes, that is true. Advanced agriculture techniques from Europe, and still the desert grows. Morocco is a small country, much smaller than Algeria or Libya, but it is two times the land of Great Britain. And everywhere it is sand, except for a tiny village here and there around a spring or well, far apart from each other like the stars in space. In the villages the wells are guarded by police. And in the desert . . ."

Henri paused. For a moment he was distracted, as if he had just seen something terrible down the street behind her. When he spoke again, his voice was bitter. "In the desert there are bandits who take nothing but your water. If they are caught, they are hanged as murderers. Have you ever been thirsty?"

She shrugged and ran her hand against the wet side of her empty glass. Her terrack remained in the center of the table. "I suppose," she said.

"No, no. I mean very thirsty. Let us say that you miss two meals. Then you are very hungry, yes. Your stomach hurts, you are faint. That is not so uncommon. You can remain many days without eating. But have you been so thirsty? So thirsty that you cannot take another step, you cannot even think. That is how thirsty you must be in the desert before you allow yourself the most tiny ration of water. Just a taste really, only enough amount to live and remind you that you remain thirsty. In Europe water runs from leaky faucets, washes streets, spills from fountains, am I right? Pools. Ice rinks. Water Piks. People take showers long enough to conduct sexual acts, do you know that? It is not francs that make this country rich, but its water."

Morocco, Henri went on, was a poor country. Many of its people were either malnourished or starving. Even their clothes and possessions were frail; the nation was about to crumble to powder and blow away. Cattle died. Staple crops failed. A windstorm was the only possible change in the weather. As Henri talked, his face close to hers, Nula felt herself removed to her own country, but what she saw was a seared, barren Ireland imprisoned beneath a vacuous blue sky, tumbleweeds in Wicklow, the pubs all boarded up. My poor parents, she thought, as her tongue swelled against the roof of her mouth. She raised her glass of Fanta and turned it over, but the trickle died before it reached her lips. Meanwhile, Henri's words came in a torrent. With such animation that he was levitated from his chair, he described his country's history, its Islam, its bazaars, its marvels. But always the conversation came back to water, and the lack of it.

"You know it is an impossibility to drink saltwater, am I right? But imagine yourself so thirsty that you think you can, that this impossibility is only a legality. In fact imagine that you are so thirsty that you will drink poison. No, you say, I never will, yet there it is, I place it before you in a clean glass, and you are so thirsty. A slow-acting poison. Aconite, rotenone, a concentrated solution of paraquat. You think: I will not drink it, but I am so thirsty, I will just touch my lips to the surface and wet them. I will dampen them only. And maybe you have that control. But maybe you do not. Maybe you say, then, as you wet your lips, I will take a small drink, that is all. A gulp, yes? Just one quick gulp does not harm me, you say. It is as if I pass my hand quick through a candle flame. Or you say if I do not even think about it, it will not affect me. You promise, I will never drink poison again—only this one time, and only a small, small amount."

"Well . . ." Nula began.

"And then the poison pours in your throat and you know you are lost. You even say to yourself, I have done it, I am poisoned, I might as well drink it all. The poison does not act yet, but you feel the liquid—at least the wetness—replenish your body, refill your cells, even as you die. And still you drink it."

"Never," she whispered through chapped lips.

Henri pulled away from her and sat back in his chair. He reached into the pocket of his jacket and, his hand cupped tenderly, removed several ounces of brilliant white sand. It was brighter than anything in the café, brighter than the day outside. It was not tainted by pocket lint, nor dirtied by small change. Although doing so hurt her eyes, Nula stared at it. He carefully deposited a little pile onto the table, next to the untouched glass of terrack.

"This is from the Sahara. I carry it around every day, so that I should know who I am, and what it means to be thirsty."

Without thinking, nearly in a trance (she told herself she was in a trance, but in fact she knew exactly what she was doing), she brought the terrack to her lips.

The drink was sweet. It reminded her of Bailey's.

"This isn't so bad," she admitted, but as she put the glass down she realized that it had done nothing to satisfy her thirst. Instead, the syrupy liquid coating the inside of her mouth turned sour and then bitter, and then from bitter to caustic. She needed water. She twisted around in her seat. There weren't any waiters in the dining room, only several busboys leaning against the far wall, ignoring her.

She couldn't even spit it out. The only way to kill the taste was to drink more.

"Please, take leisure and finish it," Henri said pleasantly, rising from the table. "But now I must leave."

"You're leaving?"

"You will telephone me."

"Where are you going?" she asked, nearly choking. The gummy terrack was burning the back of her throat.

"To visit my mother. Every Sunday afternoon I bring to her newspapers, and a dessert, often a chocolate *religieuse*. She loves desserts."

He extended his hand and, without thinking, she offered him hers. He swooped to it like a buzzard and kissed it. His lips were cool, moist.

"She lives in Paris?"

"Saint Denis," he said. It sounded to Nula like *sandy knee*. "She comes when she is twelve, after the war, when life is very bad in my country. Of course, in my country life is worse now. Or so we sometimes hear, or read, or believe, or dream. She never thinks to return. All time I think to go. Thank you for a very pleasant appointment. You will come to my flat. It is a *chambre de bonne*, but very nice, I believe. The morning is the best time. The most romance."

"But wait!" Nula cried.

Henri, however, just smiled and casually saluted her. Nula's face was flushed, every membrane in her mouth and nose parched, her eyes shrunk into her sockets. She heard her pulse accelerate, tapping against the inside of her ears. She tried to return the smile, but her lips were too blistered. The Moroccan left the café and disappeared into the blazing midday sun.

# The Joy and Melancholy
# Baseball Trivia Quiz

*Who holds the record for the most consecutive pitches thrown outside the strike zone?*

Red Beaumont of the Boston Braves, who threw twenty-seven in the third inning of the second game of a doubleheader against the Dodgers, July 31, 1953, in Brooklyn. Men proceeded from one sack of dust to the next in a graceful and reserved trot, unable to better simulate the dirt-raising helter-skelter of real base-running. The bases were loaded, there was motion and they remained loaded, so that the field appeared unchanged. The only measure of time was the addition of another run on the scoreboard.

Beaumont's arm felt fine and he could sense nothing wrong in his delivery. Nevertheless, he had lost the strike zone. For a lifetime it had hovered there, accommodating the shoulders and knees of thousands of batters without his conscious prompt; now the mental discipline required for its conjuration could not be found even if his life depended on it—and indeed it *was* the supports of his life that were at stake. Somehow the physical (the windup, the release, the follow-through) was no longer linked to the abstract (the idea of what constituted a proper pitch). He was a man out of control.

He stared at the plate. Three figures were poised there, nearly touching in three dissimilar crouches. His catcher had not come out to talk to him since his third walk, not even to offer him an encouraging pleasantry. Sixty feet six inches was as close as he wished to approach catastrophe. Stalling his windup, Beaumont looked around. The onrushing dusk had dissolved the faces of the spectators and the players and had muffled the infield chatter. He could not find his manager among the shrouded figures indistinctly stirring in the dugout. The bullpen was empty. With the game already out of reach, he had been abandoned, his salvation and what was left of his decent earned run average not worth the use of a reliever.

After the first walk, on four straight pitches, he had been disgusted, after the second he had been worried, after the third panicked, after the fourth heartsick, after the fifth angry (at his catcher, his manager, God, himself), and after the sixth in despair. Now these emotions were washed away, leaving him pale and cool. A lonely bird, either a pigeon or a seagull and probably lost, wheeled above the right field stands, dipped below the light stanchions, and then, as if impeded by an unnatural heaviness in the atmosphere, desperately pumped its wings to clear the upper deck. Its fleshy underside was brighter than anything in the ballpark, brighter even than the ball in the pitcher's left hand. Beaumont followed it with his eyes, and when they returned to the plate he could not understand the odd configuration of men before him any more than the bird could. He saw himself as the bird had seen him, a solitary figure on a little hill, no longer part of the elaborate structure of rules, statistics, schedules, and histories that defined the strike zone and the need to pass a ball through it.

His head down, he walked off the field and into the dugout, flipped the ball to one of the coaches, entered the clubhouse, changed into his street clothes, and left the ballpark. The passersby on Bedford Avenue did not recognize him as a ballplayer. The moment he melted into the anonymous city he experienced an unconditional release, which the Braves announced later that evening. No one ever heard from him again. When his family and friends thought of him, they imagined him without a shave and a little mad, a man without a past. No one ever again called him by his real name, which nevertheless remains in the official records of the National League.

*Who holds the record for the most bunt singles in one season?*
Joey Serapica of the St. Louis Browns, with 121 in 1938. An itinerant second baseman with no power, he had always been a good bunter—but never nearly as good as he was that year. He drove the pitchers and the infielders crazy. He'd bunt regardless of whether or not there was a man on base, regardless of the score, the inning, the number of strikes on him, or the condition of the field. He'd sometimes square around before the pitcher even released the ball, inviting the first and third basemen to charge in, and still he'd find a place to drop it.

He could, in that one extraordinary season, catch hold
of a fastball inside at the letters and lay it twenty feet up
the foul line of his choice. And it would stay there, not
rolling at all, except perhaps to bluff going foul. It
wouldn't, however, cross the chalk, and the infielders
would just stand there around it as if it were some
strange mushroom they had found growing at the lip of
the base path.

Sportswriters called it the "Serapica Poke," the way
he would reach out and jab the ball with his bat. The
term was not used with affection. Indeed, the name was
bestowed upon the maneuver to indicate that it was not
a true part of the game, as were lower-cased singles,
doubles, and home runs. The offense was that there was
no defense against it. It was as if he had found a new
way to play baseball or, even worse, some loophole in
the rules. In the same way that the introduction of a
new physical law would threaten to modify the opera-
tion of all other physical laws, Serapica's bunt singles
threatened the complex and delicate arrangement—the
exquisite balance between the batter and the team in
the field—that governed the game.

It disturbed Serapica too. For him the bunt hit was
easy, a single that needed little more than to be willed
into existence. If everyone did it—and it did not seem
beyond the strength and agility of any professional
athlete—there would be no baseball at all.

In a game shortly after the All-Star break, with his
team behind 6-0 in the ninth inning, Serapica faced
Washington's Mitchell Wilner, who was pitching a no-
hitter. The catcher started up to the mound, but Wilner

stared him back to his position. He already knew what he was going to throw. His first three pitches were very high and very away. With a 3-0 count, Serapica stepped from the box, dried his hands on his shirt, and checked the third base coach for the sign. There wasn't a single person in the ballpark who didn't know that he had been ordered to lay off the next one. Again Wilner threw well outside the strike zone, but, just as the umpire was about to tell him to take his base, Serapica leaned over the plate, nearly toppling, and intercepted the pitch. At the time, it seemed an act as malicious as the Lindbergh kidnapping.

The ball dribbled forward and then abruptly stopped. Wilner lunged off the mound, his legs pumping with the ungainliness of a toddler's. Both the catcher and the third baseman joined in the pursuit of the ball, which, even though it remained motionless, appeared to distance itself from the fielders with every step they took. Reaching to pick it up, the pitcher felt as if he were chasing it down some dangerous hole in a field that was buckling around him, under stands that were about to tip over. He fell to his knees. As he grabbed the ball, he saw Serapica cross the first base bag.

Still on his knees, but with a pitch as hard and accurate as any he had thrown that afternoon, Wilner pegged Serapica in the small of the back. The impact arched the runner's body as if it had been impaled. The ball dropped to the ground a foot away from the bag, and the 7,854 paid attendance cheered. Wilner's intent had been clear, but the Browns did not protest and the umpires ignored it. As Serapica took a small lead with the next batter approaching the plate, he himself felt that he had deserved the expanding, purpling bruise.

*What is the worst decision ever made by an umpire?*
Ed Fortunato's call on a 2–2 pitch thrown by Buster Smith of the Troy Haymakers in a home game against the Philadelphia Athletics, August 2, 1905. Fortunato said it was ball three, but it had just touched the outside corner, a perfect pitch—especially since Philadelphia's batter, Amos Zeldin, had been badly fooled on the pitch before, a lazy curve very wide of the plate. Smith scowled but neither he nor his catcher said anything: you couldn't gripe every time.

Now, however, with two out in the top of the eighth, Troy ahead six to four and an Athletic at first, the batter owned a full count. Smith was obliged to go to his fastball, a pitch he had been struggling with all afternoon. Trying too hard to keep it down, he threw it into the dirt for ball four. The Troy manager popped from the dugout and signalled for his left-handed reliever, Eckert King.

The large Sunday crowd gave Smith a big hand as he left. The fans were profoundly happy: the sun was warm on their faces, the air was fresh after a late-morning shower, and in the inning before the Haymakers had scored five runs. All season long Troy had rallied in the late innings, and going into today's action it was tied for second, only a game behind the Athletics. After years of hovering around .500, the team was in its first pennant race. The fans were ready to collect on their patience.

King's first pitch, however, was belted out of the ballpark, startling a few pedestrians on Carthage Road. As Bobbo Miller, the Athletics' cleanup hitter, trotted around the bases behind his two teammates, the stands were virtually silent, as if the spectators were consulting their rule books to determine how to score a ball that clears the outfield fence by twenty feet. Then there was a dark, fevered murmur.

On the playing field, the Troy Haymakers grimly paced around their positions. King would have gladly taken back the excellent season he had been having if he could have also taken back that last hanging curve. What hurt the players was not the size of the home run, nor even the fact that it put the team back in the hole, 7-6. What hurt, what stung, was the knowledge that they should have been out of the inning with the previous batter.

Fortunato himself felt a little sick, a little tired of umpiring. He had realized his mistake as soon as he called the ball; he had whispered a prayer that it would not be fateful. He wished that he could be replaced by some unerring engine, a mechanical referee.

Meanwhile, the worst thought that could enter a sportsman's mind percolated through the team's collective consciousness: the game's outcome was predestined, as was the outcome of the entire season. In their last turn at bat the Haymakers went quietly, as if they were down not by one run but by fourteen. In the first inning of the first game of a road trip the following Tuesday, the Haymakers' best pitcher gave up five consecutive base hits. The team went on to lose six in a row, dropping out of the pennant race like a stone, and finished with its worst record in seven years. The players were demoralized, slowly taking a sullen faith in the idea that it took something less tangible than hits and good pitching to win, and whatever it was, they didn't have it and couldn't get it, ever. They forgot the game with Philadelphia; the awful losses that followed were what seared their memories that winter and the following season.

Around the same time the fans quietly decided that they had overestimated not only the Haymakers, but baseball itself. Their hopes, their passions, and their carefully drawn evaluations of the team's abilities had proven dependent on a mirage. They had been suckered. It was a stupid, cruel game, which owed less to calculable talent than to the merciless whims of fate. After peaking in 1905, the annual attendance to Troy's home games fell in each succeeding year.

Soon all that was left were a few fanatics, men whose partisanship was insincere. They knew nothing about baseball. When they cheered the Haymakers, they were really only cheering themselves for having the romantic notion of attending a ball game and rooting for the home team. Troy schoolboys, more exacting in their allegiances, were likely to find it easier to name all the players on the New York Giants than to name the Haymakers' starting nine. Only 72,000 paying fans entered Troy Memorial Park in 1908, and that winter the team traded all its players, changed its name, and moved to another city.

*What is the worst trade of players ever made by two teams?*
The trade made on March 11, 1931, between the
Petrozavodsk Boilermakers and the Aix-en-Provence
Bantams. The two teams had been fierce rivals since
the beginning of history, always close in the standings,
either vying for the American League pennant or trying
to climb over each other out of the cellar. They had
developed distinctive styles of play, the Boilermakers
known for their big innings and intimidating pitchers,
while Aix went for the gonfalon with the hit-and-run,
the timely base hit up the middle, and great defensive
play. Fueled by geographic proximity—the two cities
glowered at each other from opposite banks of the
Missouri—the baseball rivalry came to define the cities
themselves. With their breweries and slaughterhouses,
the Aixers thought of themselves as more refined than
the Petrozavodsk polloi, whose brute force mined the
coal and forged the steel that brought the city its wealth.
The intensity of their rivalry was renowned, supplying
newspaper feature columns throughout the country
with tales of fans who fasted and grew beards during
losing streaks, places of worship that held special services before important games between the two teams,
barroom brawls in faraway Cathay and Patagonia over
the teams' respective merits, and even the Petrozavodsk
man who bludgeoned his wife to death for making an
admiring remark about an Aix pitcher's pick-off move to
first, and then the local jury that refused to convict him.
   Even for those citizens who took little notice of the
baseball teams that campaigned in their name, for
whom baseball itself was a time-wasting pursuit, the city

across the river held a dread fascination. One could see it from the waterfront, shimmering in the haze. Despite the lurid reports that made their way into the national press, a commercial traveler from one city who found himself in the other did not necessarily risk some terrible prank or indignity upon his person. Yet his disorientation was acute, as if he were walking the streets of some kind of dream city, the sidewalk spongelike and the skyscrapers on a tilt, a place that existed in the physical world only in the sense that it was not the other place. Going about his business, riding the streetcar, buying a cigar, even breathing the local air, the traveler might feel himself a bit of a traitor, or even unsure that it was really himself doing these things. He hurried home.

The rivalry went on for years and decades until a mild late-winter afternoon that promised spring, when the streets of both cities rang with the high-pitched cries of newsboys peddling extras. The news was this: Each team had traded all its players to the other, an even swap.

In the first half hour, hardly anyone would buy the papers, not believing that they were "for real." Then the outraged fans turned on the newsboys, nearly lynching one of them in Aix until the police restored order.

The citizens of each city did not know what to make of the news, once it was confirmed by the teams' front offices. Men furrowed their brows around beer taps. Fathers took their sons for long, stone-kicking walks, their arms on the boys' shoulders. The two teams' owners, an Aix rail magnate and a Petrozavodsk steel tycoon, had reached agreement in secret, without consulting their business partners or the press, and as it turned out, the arrangement was more complicated than the newspapers first reported. Certain business interests of the two were also exchanged, other assets consolidated, recapitalized, or eliminated; a foundry was involved; so was a railroad right-of-way and a bank. The ballplayers were in fact a minor consideration, a throw-in at the last minute. The newspapers could not determine which of the plutocrats got the better deal.

Fate had decreed that the two teams would open the 1931 season in Aix's Charlemagne Field. The game was sold out and the ferry from Petrozavodsk had to augment its schedule, but the fans who filed into the ballpark that day were subdued and wary, at odds with themselves, as if unsure what kind of sporting event they had come to see. They gingerly took their seats, shoulder-to-shoulder with the other city's fans. When the Aix team, composed entirely of players who until a few weeks earlier had been Petrozavodsk Boilermakers—even the manager, coaches and batboys had been traded—took their defensive positions, there was a scattering of applause and boos, all of it tentative. The fans asked themselves for whom had they rooted all these years: the abstraction called a "home team" or its tangible constituent parts?

Here, scraping the foreign dirt around first base with his cleats, was Emil Hockstader, the powerful right-handed cleanup hitter who had led the Boilermakers to the pennant three times in the past decade. He was wearing Aix's red, blue, and white. Coming to the plate was Hector Sauvage, the base-churning leadoff hitter and base stealer that had bedeviled a generation of Petrozavodsk catchers. Just the year before, in an incident burned into the hearts of Petrozavodsk fans, he had slid hard into the Boilermakers' second baseman and was led off the field under police protection. Now he wore the Petrozavodsk traveling grays.

The trade was an abomination, of course. A non-sequitur. An overthrow of the natural order. But there it was, for all to see, on the newly manicured basepaths and lush green outfield. Further questions nagged at the fans. How did the virtues of a ballplayer transmit itself to the city for which he played, or vice versa? How could our heroes win glory for the other side as they had for us? Why was it "good" when the home team won?

In subsequent years, some fans continued to root for their favorite players in the opposite city, sometimes even when they played against the fans' own home team; others deferred, minimized, or reversed their support during those particular games. Other fans maintained their partisanship in favor of their reconstituted home team, perhaps developing a dislike for the departed, once-beloved players by dwelling on those professional traits that had once secretly irritated them, the hitch in the swing, the insolent home run trot. But few fans were as passionate as they had been, and their sense of their hometowns' distinctiveness gradually faded until the two cities' expanding peripheries merged into a single suburban sprawl, and the cities themselves dissolved into the river's mists.

*What was the last American League stadium to install lights for night games after it was built?*

Harmon Field in Detroit, in 1948. The move was reluctant. Although he announced that the introduction of night baseball was made out of "economic necessity," the stadium's owner, Walter J. Harmon, could not understand, despite the explanations of his front office staff, what those necessities were. He continued to maintain, even in public, that the sport was "meant to be played in the daylight."

Horace Watkins, a veteran baseball reporter covering the first night game for the following afternoon's issue of the Detroit *Independent*, agreed, especially as the new lighting system had not yet been extended to the press box. Did anyone care whether he wrote his story?

In fact, all the stands were near dark, the fans invisible, their cheers part of the ether, like static. Nor could Watkins see the other writers upstairs with him, except for the occasional incandescence at the end of a cigar or cigarette and the reflection of the lit field on a pair of eyeglasses. The few comments they made during the course of the game arrived in his vicinity disembodied, nearly inaudible.

The field, however, was as bright as day; no, it was much brighter. It glowed as if its light were coming not from the arc lamps suspended above his head, but from beneath a translucent skin. The grass and the infield dirt radiated their colors from garish, heretofore invisible, regions of the spectrum. Nothing was real. The ballfield's measures were hemmed by the moth-filled night, with the left fielder lost beyond the edge of the dark. The features of the players were difficult to distinguish in the glare, and the relentless light destroyed their shadows, robbing them of dimension and substance. Running around on the flat, foreshortened field, the athletes were mere schematics, electrified ghosts, as if—Watkins realized years later, after Harmon Field was torn down, lights and all, and the *Independent* had folded—the game were being played on a television screen.

*Who holds the record for the most balls fouled off in a single at bat?*

Chuck Murry of the Seattle Pilots, with fifty-six in his only plate appearance in the major leagues, September 28, 1969. Now a part-owner of a Ford dealership in Vancouver, Murry sometimes wakes after midnight in his completely darkened room next to his wife, who in sleep smells like warm bread. For a few moments he lies there disconcerted. He knows he's at home and in bed, but it seems that he is also back in Seattle's now-demolished Sicks Stadium, the one-day, one big league chance given him after he'd kicked around the minors for eight years not yet exhausted. He cannot make out the bedroom but he can feel the tape around the bat handle and the dirt under his cleats.

Distracted by the crowd and his own overheated awareness of where he was, he had taken the first pitch, the best he would ever see again, for a strike. The next two balls, sophisticated sliders, were well outside, but he almost went after them, eliciting a tiny, wicked smile from the pitcher, Wallace Porter. He laid off the fourth pitch, a strike at the knees, and then realized he was nearly back in the dugout without having swung his bat. Smelling his eagerness, Porter crossed him up next on a change-up, but Murry hung on and dribbled the ball left of the third base line, determined to survive.

Indeed, the rookie now dug himself into the batter's box as if it were a foxhole, swinging at everything he could reach, fouling twenty-one consecutive pitches into the net protecting the fans behind the plate, Reserved Admission, the Pilots' dugout, the press box, down the runway into the clubhouse, at the first base coach, and against the toes of the home plate umpire. "C'mon, straighten it out," shouted someone from his own team, less encouraging than impatient. The umpire swore after he was hit, and not at the blind chance of such a mishap but at Murry himself. The batter, however, was enjoying his cuts. He was disappointed when Porter, tiring, nearly threw wild and he had to take ball three.

Even with a full count Murry hacked at everything thrown at him, hitting each pitch. He popped up balls that cleared the height of the stadium and returned three rows into the box seats, forcing the catcher into fruitless wrestling matches with the paying customers. He smoked a liner against the rolled rain tarp, which responded with a pained thud. He slammed Porter's forty-first offering 450 feet into the roped-off area of the upper deck, just inches from the foul pole. The ball rattled around like a loose part until a boy sprinting from the $1.25 section behind third pried it from another in a desperate tussle under the folded seats. Murry was still watching them, wondering why they were not in school, when the next pitch came. He casually fouled it behind him, hardly even looking at it.

He had stopped thinking about getting a base hit or striking out, or even of putting the ball in play. He expected to foul off balls to the end of time, forever drawing from the stadium's supply (the management would have to call for more), forever dispensing souvenirs of this historic event among the game's spectators. Time had stopped; each foul ball further dilated the moment. He was no longer tense or in any way muddled. In fact, he saw (and now often recalls) everything: a blister above the first baseman's lips, the batboy kneeling by the rack, a pretty woman in the season boxes who looked like his own mother had when he was younger.

It was a cool, autumn afternoon, more the season for football. Shadows had overtaken the playing field, and all that was left of summer (Apollo 11, Woodstock) was a brilliant bolt of light against the sparsely populated stands in right field. A pale, vitreous moon rose over the scoreboard. There are still afternoons like this in Pompeii, Massachusetts, where Murry had grown up. Three thousand miles west, he could taste (slapping the ball to the left of the leaping third baseman) the air seared by drying leaves and hear (slamming it against the catcher's mask) the last-minute assignations made by students in the high school parking lot.

Each memory is telescoped inside another, as all would be at the end of life and, if the world of living things is lucky, as our lives would be left to us in death: remembering remembering remembering, and so on. Murry was astonished when Porter's sixty-second pitch passed through his bat, emerging on the other side of it into the catcher's glove. The pop sounded like a champagne bottle being opened, and he recalled a New Year's Eve that had not yet come. "All right," said the umpire. "Get your ass out of here." Murry, however, does not recall the return to the dugout, and as sleep gently retakes him, his memory turns back in confusion to the thought that the at bat would last forever. A happy man, he curls his body around that of his wife, as if he were crowding the plate.

# Cats in Space

For reasons that had become unknown, a large number of cats occupied the otherwise orderly suburban neighborhood in which I grew up. They belonged to no one and were fed by no one, yet they proliferated the way roaches did elsewhere. None had names, except those that distinguished them by their defects: One Eye, Torn Ear, Limpo. They knocked over garbage cans, tore up gardens, and shrieked across the night. They were unloved, even by the sweetest of the block's littlest kids. My across-the-street neighbor, Ricky Brennan, shot BBs at them from his bedroom window.

Every spring, as if by ancient tradition, Nathan Wasserman's older brother Mark would visit the places where we had discovered litters the previous few weeks, under porches and in garages. He'd tear the kittens from their mothers two or three at a time and toss them into a brown paper supermarket bag, scrupulously using one bag per litter. Then he'd tie the bag closed with a piece of twine. The mother cats were too phlegmatic to offer opposition, hardly even hissing. They had, like us, become accustomed to the routine.

Mark would put the bags in his father's car, we'd pile in, and without saying a word he'd drive us to the shallow body of water we called either the pond, the swamp, or the sump, about three quarters of a mile away. It was large—we could have called it a lake—but it appeared to be fed only by the dregs of beer bottles tossed in from cars parked on the secluded, unlit strip of road that grazed it on the way to the next suburban subdivision. The pond never looked clean, or like water at all. Its liquid thick and oily, on humid days the pond sweated the odor of mothballs. Fathers sometimes brought their very young kids there and, with a hook and a line, allowed them to pretend to fish.

Once every spring five or six of us would lean against the car while Mark carried the shopping bags to the pond's edge. As he picked up the bags, the kittens inside became frantic, now crying, now snarling, now moaning, now crying again. Mark showed neither pleasure nor discomfort at his task, nor even that he noticed the animal commotion in his hands. We admired him for this, though as we got older we discovered that his cool was in fact a kind of dullness and he became something of a joke. Mark would step to the water's edge and without ceremony fling the sacks about twenty feet into the pond. They spun end over end a few times and then made an odd, tinny, unwatery splash. One or two of the bags might resurface for a moment. The mewls of the drowning kittens, clearly heard from where we stood, were wonderfully terrifying, the authentic song of death.

Although one couldn't swim in the pond, it was a frequent make-out site for our older brothers and, incredibly, our older sisters. A line of parked cars fronted the pond every weekend and summer night. Once there was a "drought," or at least a couple of hot months of infrequent rainfall. The pond didn't dry up completely, but the level fell, revealing tire husks, encrusted auto-mobile batteries, corroded bicycle frames, and empty paint cans. One afternoon that summer I walked along the water's edge with a few of my friends. They believed they would find used condoms in the cracked mud. I myself was looking for bags of dead kittens, bags I expected to number in the hundreds. I didn't discover any, which made me wonder if they had somehow dissolved. My friends didn't find any condoms.

The drownings only limited the growth of the cat population: there were always more than enough to go around for various entertainments and scientific experiments, most of which tested their ability to land on their feet. We threw quite a few cats off Billy Osinski's roof as, over the years, these experiments became increasingly sophisticated. Five of us, each with a cheap snapshot camera against his face, once lined up alongside the house, while Osinski held the subject cat over our heads. Then he let it drop and, as documentation for a science fair project that would never be completed, we took the animal's photograph at each stage of its descent. It landed on its feet, smashed its snout against the cement, and then slinked away, sneezing. Each sneeze sprayed a fine crimson mist.

One Saturday afternoon when I was eleven or twelve, we chipped in for a bunch of thirty-five-cent helium balloons at a nearby five-and-ten. At home I removed a half-gallon cardboard container of milk from the fridge, emptied the milk into a pickle jar from under the sink, and cut away the carton's top. We stapled the carton to the strings hanging from the balloons, thus fashioning a little gondola. Then we debated our choice for the craft's passenger.

"It should be the smartest one," Nathan said. "Like the way they pick the astronauts. You know, give them tests."

"What's the difference?" I said. "They're cats."

"We should get the smallest," decided Osinski. "So it won't escape."

None of us could have said exactly where we hoped to send the animal, though balloon launchings had a long history in our neighborhood. We often tied messages with our addresses to them, in the hope that we'd get a response from some distant country. There was never any letter from abroad, however, nor even a phone call from Syosset—so we probably didn't expect to see the cat again. But then the dogs that the Russians launched into space didn't come back either. According to the television, they burned up in the atmosphere. Perhaps we thought our cat would do the same.

We eventually found a young tortoiseshell that had evaded Mark's culling. Although the kitten was free of visible defects, it was an ugly animal, with metallic green eyes and a wiry, uncuddly body. Nathan wanted to whirl it around in a bucket, to prepare it for the g-forces, but Osinski noted that gas was leaking from the balloons. Already two of them were slumping toward the ground.

We cut slits in the gondola's sides so that the kitten could see out. "Where is it going to pee?" Nathan's little sister Eleanor asked, obliging us to cut a hole in the corner of the carton. The kitten complained when we picked it up, but once it was placed in the gondola it satisfied itself by sniffing at the milk-encrusted walls. I gave it a piece of lox, as provisions for the trip, but the animal ate it immediately and whined for more. We ended up giving the kitten all that was left in the fridge. It tore at the fish as we carried the balloons out to the middle of the street.

Perhaps as many as eight of us met there as if by prearrangement, or destiny. We were mostly quiet, and each incidental remark or joke went unanswered. Since we had brought home the balloons, the day had turned bitter, and we were now impatient to get back indoors. Just as we were about to let it go, the kitten stuck its face through the hole we had cut. It let out a series of short, uniform, almost electronic mews. Nathan poked its face away with his finger and told it, "Get ready for blastoff." It returned to the hole and resumed crying.

Its cries did not change their tempo or tone as the balloons rose. For the first minute or so, the craft's ascent was slow, almost imperceptible. Then the wind picked up and it gained altitude. The cat's cries diminished until nearly inaudible, but not quite.

We ourselves didn't speak. There had been a moment of elation when the gondola cleared our heads, but now we didn't even smile. "Catch," Osinski said, palming a football, but no one took up the offer. We just looked into the sky. Once in a while the wind caught a sound like that of rusty hinges or worn brakes.

For a long time the balloons didn't appear to move. They just hung there, the gondola the size of the full moon. I entertained the belief that it would always be there, as a kind of punishment, the cat over our heads, mewling as we walked to and from school, played spongeball, and grew up and got married.

Yet I felt no relief when Nathan announced, "It's coming down." A gust of chill wind blew grit into our eyes. When our eyes cleared, we saw that Nathan was right: the apparent size of the gondola was a little greater than it had been a minute earlier. One of the balloons had lost most of its helium and hung off the milk carton like a shriveled, broken flower.

The balloons descended much more slowly than they had risen, blown gently past our block. We ran through the Rosettis' backyard and pushed ourselves through the hedges onto the property of the house on the next street. The cat, however, had lost no more than a little altitude. Not yet ready to land, it sailed over the next block and the block after that. We fell back through the hedges, claimed our English racers and stingrays, and took off after it.

Our housing development was a labyrinth of "drives,' "lanes," and "ways" that twisted around each other, so that the gondola hovered at our shoulders and behind our backs as we furiously pedaled after it. Several times it disappeared behind a house or a stand of trees. We emerged at last from the development, at the shore of the pond, just as the balloons were skimming over the pond's surface. As soon as the gondola touched the surface, its forward motion was arrested, and it fell in.

We bicycled to the edge of the muck and dismounted quietly. I made a conscious effort not to look at my

friends. Instead I stared across the pond, watching a spot
a little short of where the gondola was sinking.

Osinski finally broke the silence. He said, "Glub, glub,
glub."

I let my bicycle drop to the ground and waded in,
still wearing my dungarees and sneakers. The slime
was warm and oily, and when it touched my crotch
I shivered. My feet slipped on various things on the
pond-bed—rocks, tires, broken beer bottles, probably
condoms, probably dead cats. It took me about forty-five
seconds to get to the gondola, which had tipped to its
side away from me. My motion pushed it for a moment
out of my reach and nearly turned it over. When finally
I got there I found the kitten huddled in a corner of the
carton, drooling from fear. It hissed and extended its
claws as I grabbed its scruff.

I returned, my friends watching me without expression on their faces, Nathan and Osinski with their arms
crossed. I thought of the dead, who from another shore
watched the living in eternal silence. I put the kitten
down. I don't know what I expected, but all it did was
whimper a few times and then interrupt itself to vigor-
ously scratch its left ear. Holding it against my handle-
bars, I brought it back to our neighborhood, even
though there was no man, woman, child, or beast who
would have missed it.

The cat didn't show any ill effects from the flight, nor
even any recollection of it. It did, however, remember
the lox, and after that it never strayed far from our back
door.

I never quite adopted the cat, and never named it,

but it more or less became mine, and years later when I went to college, I took it with me. Now fat and old, and always dissatisfied with its food, the cat surreptitiously lived in my dorm for a year and a half. By that time I had gone through several roommates unhappy with the odor of its litter box under my desk, and I myself would have been pleased to get rid of the animal. Then one wet Saturday afternoon it died.

It was a peculiar time in my life. The cat died, and I had to take it to a vet just to dispose of the body. Two weeks later I broke up with my girlfriend, cruelly, for almost no reason except to see what it would be like, and a month after that I dropped out of school. I felt this enormous freedom—I was an adult!—but had no idea what to do with it, and I ended up working the next three years for a travel agency.

I now infrequently return to the neighborhood, which is mostly inhabited by strangers. The descendants of the cats we knew still roam its nights, but there seems to be fewer of them, and I wonder if I overestimated their numbers when I was a child. The pond has been filled in and replaced by a very small shopping center that, to judge by its empty storefronts and cracked parking lot, will soon be abandoned. I am married now, with my own children, and I have a job that sometimes requires brutality, in a quiet, nine-to-five way. I take my children to parks, watch TV with them, and help them with their homework. I try to be sure they are kind to animals, but you can never be sure of anything. Like the rest of us, they're on their own.

# The Republic of St. Mark, 1849

"Many discoveries which we laugh at as childish
and fantastic later vindicate themselves."
—An eyewitness.

A lessandro Cacciaguida has been dying all his life,
indeed from the moment of conception, but in the
last week he has died more than in all the preceding
weeks of his life, and in the last day more than in all the
preceding days. In a matter of hours his fall to the earth
will be completed, and he will be a body at rest. Charles
Albert has abandoned the Republic. Marshal Haynau
holds all passage to our city. Cholera has left corpses rotting in the gutters and floating in the canals, and who-
ever among Venice's living has the strength to eat does
not have any food. Now what is required of the enemy
is patience.

All the members of Alessandro's household are either
dead or gone from the city; he does not recall their individual fates. Of his servants, the last to remain was
Maria, his wife's maid. Maria died two nights before,
while he was washing her befouled body he had once so
lightly enjoyed. Now he walks through his house for the
last time, virtually a ghost, running his hands along the
spines of his books, an oil painting of his son, and a small

escritoire that was given to him by an ancestor and will soon be either hacked to bits or sold to some Viennese merchant who has no known ancestor of his own. His head spinning, Alessandro passes from the house and his courtyard, too feeble to shut a door or gate.

If some bandit laid a dagger in his chest, then Alessandro would at least see his killer's eyes. Now, he is being slain invisibly by the Venetian businessmen who have maneuvered our city into fighting this war without allies, the Venetian politicians whose ineptitude at diplomacy is surpassed only by their ineptitude at war, the Austrian generals who have never seen his face, and this dread wasting disease that turns a man into shit.

Alessandro's house is on a shady lane; the coolness under the trees mocks his fever. The lane opens onto the Campo San Angelo, which is as deserted as it might have been three hours before dawn a year ago. A dog noses a pile of offal. Something smaller scurries from one gutter to the other. All the shops are padlocked. Alessandro rests against a cool, whitewashed wall. He thinks, well, this is where I will die, after a lifetime of speculation about the place and the date, in the Campo San Angelo, against a wall belonging to Girolamo Biaggio, whose family has known mine for three hundred years, and who hasn't spoken to me in two, because of a dispute about a patch of weedy pasture near Mestre. Alessandro cannot remember today's date, but believes the month is August. At that moment, with a shout and guffaw, three or five stocky youths appear, in ragged uniforms, jostling each other on the narrow sidewalk like billiard balls. They are in an ugly humor.

As savage as the enemy has proven himself to be, worse has been the invasion of mercenaries from throughout Italy, soldiers without an army, loitering about our streets, ostensibly on our behalf. If there is a demonstration in favor of republicanism, they are at hand; a half hour later they are carrying the banner of the Piedmontese; an hour after that, they are emptying the taverns of provisions. They are angry, for this has not been the war they were promised. It is a siege, one in which the enemy, because of the contagion, remains so distant his ships can be seen only from the highest structures of the city. So the soldiers haunt our streets, looking for another fight.

Alessandro, too weak to fight a cat for a morsel of liver, turns away, looking at the ground, hoping that if he doesn't see them, they will not see him. They approach, their boots clicking against the street. The heel of one of their boots is loose, causing a slight echo with each step. The mercenaries pass without incident, and Alessandro looks at their backs, not relieved at all, but a little saddened by his invisibility.

The Austrians and their Croatian troops are also dying of fever and have been forced to leave their positions, but from the safety of their ships they have devised new strategies against us, each more marvelous than the one before. In the unfettered republican press, there has been speculation about self-propelled cannons, underwater boats that can glide unseen up the Grand Canal, and ice machines that will suffocate the city in a summer blizzard of snow. A few weeks ago a new rumor spread through Venice: Haynau was planning to attack the city from the air. This was a bit of relief, comedy amid the cholera. Immediately the city was placarded. A cartoon showed the promised event: a mustachioed Croat atop a balloon, dropping a bomb onto the Piazza San Marco. Other caricatures were offered in broadsheets and newspapers. There were many jokes made; pedestrians teased each other by suddenly stopping and staring into the sky, as if they had caught the first glimpse of these engines of destruction. On the following day, July 12, the holiday of the Madonna della Salute, the comedy came true. A small number of balloons appeared above the Austrians' anchor. They rose very slowly, like puffs of very dense smoke, and many fell back into the water.

Alessandro was in the Piazzetta at the time, having come from an interview with Manin. What were the President of the Republic's intentions? Would he impose bread rationing? Would he attempt a civilian evacuation? Would he ask for assistance from Mazzini or Garibaldi? Did he have any plan at all for breaking the siege? Manin just smiled, as if he knew the answers to these questions, but thought it clever not to answer them. As Alessandro returned home, reflecting that the hero-democrat of one year would be the fool-despot of the next, the Austrians seemed to be making their own reply to his questions by sending their ridiculous devices over the Lagoon.

If the Austrians thought this strategy would terrorize our city, they were mistaken. We can imagine, of course, such a reaction of superstitious wonderment in some Bosnian backwater, but here in Venice we are well acquainted with the *montgolfière* as a Parisian entertainment. Indeed, our citizens met the supposed instruments of their doom with a cheer—previously, there had been little cause for cheer—and mothers pointed out the objects to their children, who were dressed in ribbons and bows for the holiday. None of the balloons reached the city. A few fell near the Lido and one into the castle at St. Andrew. Attached to them was some kind of grenade, which damaged neither person nor structure.

Now, today, spared by the mercenaries, Alessandro staggers from Biaggio's wall. He will, evidently, die some-place else. He advances along Calle Bognolo in the direction of San Marco, stopping at frequent intervals. When the siege began, the city was already depopulated. The wealthy and well connected had received advance word of the Austrians' approach. As for himself, Alessandro knew that the city was threatened, but he did nothing to protect his person or his household, not out of courage or patriotism, but out of indolence. Or did he too put all his faith in the Republic, in the President, now the beloved Dictator, Manin?

With the citizens gone, the dogs have come out, and they slink along the walls and into the yards. The dogs are mangy—presumably, the more appetizing ones have been eaten—but they are not thin. They've found food, somehow. Perhaps the Austrians have contrived a way to feed them, in order to taunt us.

There are fires this morning. Black smoke plumes over rooftops from three distant quarters. The fire department, led by Manin himself, will rush to put them out, but not before more citizens are left homeless.

Manin has forbidden priests to ring handbells on their way to administer last rites; he fears the din might panic the population. Instead silence looms over the city, a thundercloud of hopelessness.

On the door of a bakery, Alessandro sees a sign: "This shop is closed because of the death of its proprietor." Scrawled on the wall alongside that, he reads: "Viva La Republica!" and "Viva Manin!"

There is human feces in the street: the dogs sniff it for the most intimate scents of their masters, and then trot away. The excrement is runny, sour smelling, and entirely different from the excrement of other animals, Alessandro thinks. It is a shade less dark. Here on the next street is more shit, though firmer—and recognizably a man's, showing a faithful model of his entrails. Alessandro considers the following: that each animal evacuates in a particular way, depending on the size and shape of its anus and the strength and contours of the muscles that deliver the excretion. Perhaps in the future doctors will invent an entire medicine based on fecal measurements, a discipline to rival phrenology.

It is on the next street that he sees his friend Donatello Bartini, who is married to his cousin Celia. Bartini is on his stomach, one of his arms splayed beneath him. Alessandro thinks of the many kindnesses Bartini has shown him in the past; he can recall his high-pitched, easy laugh.

The best life is the one that prepares you best for death. This is the life in which you gradually lose your ties to the earth: those to your parents, your siblings and cousins, your wife, your children, your comrades.

Rather than being struck down when you feel yourself to be most loved, it is better to lose your teeth, your hair, your eyesight, and then your loved ones and thus for your body to lose weight in increments, so that in the end you barely disturb the soil of the earth you tread. This is what has happened to Alessandro in the last few days, losing everything, but fortunately in such a fashion that he can hardly recall his former health and prosperity. Now he is ready to die. The angels of death shall come and he will set a place at his table for them.

A number of citizens have congregated at the Piazza, but they make no demonstration. They do not speak, not to Alessandro nor to each other. Occasionally, one of them looks up at Manin's offices. They are humiliated. They have placed all their hopes in Manin, in the Republic, in democracy—that is, in themselves, and they have discovered themselves wanting.

And it is now that Alessandro sees the first of the balloons since the Madonna della Salute, dropping slowly down the front of the dictator's palace. It precipitates at his feet, a taffeta sack about an arm's length across, open at the bottom, where, attached to the bag by some stiff wire, is a brazier. A string from this assembly dangles below it to a little cotton bag. The bag spills open as it alights onto the pavement. He recognizes its contents immediately: gunpowder. Alessandro tries to laugh at the dreamy ingenuousness of this invention, but there is no breath in his lungs. As he seats himself in the street, a gust of wind lifts the package away and skitters it across the cobblestones.

Alessandro remains. Who knows how long he lies

there? He sleeps, but he does not dream. An animal, perhaps a dog, sniffs his crotch. Someone murmurs a few words over his head. He listens to them without comprehension. The words are Latin, but the speaker employs an entirely different language, in which these words mean something other than what they do in Latin. When Alessandro awakes, his body is stiff from the awkwardness of his position.

He stands, unsteadily. He wonders if he has left the house without his walking stick. He is convinced that some Croat has taken it.

He thinks he must now cross the city one more time. And he comes upon such trifling sights as rats the size of cattle, cats dressed in the Milan fashion playing bassoons while driving by in a four-by-four pulled by archbishops, angels in meal sacks, and his sister, whom he buried just last week. She says, "There are lamb chops in my chamber pot." He kisses her on her lips; her breath tastes of anise. Several canals have been drained, and in the muck Alessandro sees the skeletons of his family and neighbors, some of which have lain there for centuries. Underneath the bones lie the roofs of the buildings of another city. Vienna perhaps.

In the Campo San Luca, Alessandro passes friends. They stare at him, horrified. Alfredo Scitelli sputters, "I dreamed that you were dead." In fact, Alessandro knows that Alfredo is dead, but he politely replies, "I'm honored." In Venice, of course, not all the suffering is done by men and women. For example, the still-red roses in the Contessa's window box are being driven mad by the screams of her rotting gardenias.

A second balloon floats down to Alessandro's feet. Others drift over the tops of the city, and he is glad to have lived long enough to see them, for this is a view well into the next century. The smoke he saw earlier was from the fires set by the balloons . . . Frederick gains no tactical advantage over our army. This is warfare against the populace: much more effective, and fitting, for we are a democracy and it is we free citizens who should pay for the follies of our government. Someday democracy will reign throughout Italy, all men will be victims, and all men will be held responsible.

In Paris last year free citizens chased Louis-Philippe to England; Metternich soon joined him there. Kossuth declared Hungarian independence. In Prague, Pavlacki organized a Slav Congress. In Berlin, rebels armed with paving stones battled troops. Frederick was forced to bombard Vienna itself. In Milan, the Austrians were re-pelled with military props taken from La Scala. But now the Austrians are coming back.

How beautiful, how graceful, these sacks of flame. On the next block one lands upon a pile of refuse. A smile crosses the loose skin of Alessandro's face, which feels when he rubs it as if it were about to fall off his skull. The brazier lights the refuse, but the fire does not spread to the gunpowder, and Alessandro stands by it, savoring the odor of burning garbage.

He sees the future: these devices can be perfected to travel great distances, so that the Austrians can lay waste to our cities without ever leaving their country. This is a major advance in warfare, which can now pro-ceed without morally implicating the combatants. In the future, generals will eradicate whole cities while sipping their tea or writing memoirs about battles they will win after their own deaths.

Alessandro watches the balloons in their unhurried descent. Some interrupt their fall and, buoyed by a gust twisting around the square, return to the skies. He reaches out to touch one. As he does so, the cords that hang from it lean toward him and embrace and gently lift his desiccated body off its feet. He is not surprised by this, not even a little: everything since the first day of the siege has been wonderful—terrifying and wonderful.

The first moments of his ascent are vertiginous. While the balloon carries him off the ground very slowly, the cobblestones appear to rush away beneath his feet with great velocity. He thinks he sees himself being lifted; then he thinks he sees himself being left behind. For a few seconds or so, he can stretch his leg and tap the ground with his slippers, but then almost suddenly he is high enough above the pavement to fear being dashed against it. But he is not afraid.

From his height, three times as high now as, say, the San Marco campanile, Venice appears untouched by war. Here and there fires smolder, but otherwise the scene is sunnily placid. Alessandro sees the Austrians' positions: there is a gun emplacement at Campalto, another on San Giuliano, ships all around the Lagoon. They've taken Fort Malghera; near Malghera is a novel construction, a set of cannons being mounted on a bed of timber, their breeches sunk into the earth to give them optimal elevation, and thus the greatest range. What a spy he would make, if only he could communicate his discoveries to the military command, if only we still possessed a military command. A few cattle graze on the mainland; a vessel rests at anchor. Alessandro understands now that height is the advantage of the future, that in the next century or in the century after that, men will live in lofty towers flush against the sky, from which they will occasionally fall with terrific impact, making courtyards thrillingly dangerous places. Great armies of men will erect these towers, transforming the face of the earth, while they themselves remain wretched and ill used. And just as these balloons can carry bags of gunpowder, they can also carry armies, from one ocean to the next, from Africa to China, mixing bloods and languages, so that in the future the entire race of man will speak a single tongue, but this tongue will express nothing of importance. Wars, of course, will take place in the sky, as armies rush to conquer one cloud after another.

The cities of the future have already been built in the clouds; we may see their spires upon the rush of dusk in summer. Alessandro passes up through a cumulous boulevard. In the clouds the canals are filled with stones, over which gondoliers pull wheeled carts filled with water. The hot air that lifts the balloons of the Austrians powers the engines of the cloud cities, and in these cities the temperature of the streets is therefore several degrees warmer than what we are accustomed to, causing winters of warm, wet rain and miasmatic summers. Citizens pay to have their homes chilled or, to avoid the plagues brought by hot, close places, they sleep out on the streets without homes altogether. In the clouds, the buildings have multiplied in number and size, so that even a greengrocer's is as great as a cathedral on the earth. Alessandro looks at his arm and, as it has taken on the ethereal properties of the higher spheres, he can see through his skin the sheath of blood that lines the inside of his body and the quicksilver shimmer of his soul.

Here in the sky all objects are dissolved of their physical substance; their intrinsic nature is visible, revealing not only the souls of men but those of inanimate objects. What makes a boat a boat or a house a house becomes apparent above the clouds. Alessandro wanders through libraries of pageless, coverless books, each of the volumes simply the idea itself, shorn of words.

There are two realms, the earth and the sky, and laws that operate in one are void in the other. For example, the earth draws objects made of earth to earth—men, buildings, their tools—while the sky draws objects made of the sky to the sky. These include vapor, the hot air that lifts the Austrians' balloons, and the human spirit. On earth we speak of cause and effect, implying that one follows the other. This is not true in the sky, where all effects are preordained, and the heavens wheel and blaze in an effort to propagate the cause—Alessandro's death was long foretold, but only now can his killer be determined. In the heavens, angels float on milk, which comes from the tears of plants that grow in the dust between the stars, which are really little holes in the celestial dome through which spills the radiance of God.

In this sphere rivers flow uphill, night is lit and day is dark, the righteous prosper, bodies at rest tend to travel in eccentric circles, finches speak Dutch, children give birth to their fathers (but not to their mothers), and over a candle flame water turns to an ice that reflects your future. The moon is made of this ice, and it reflects the pock-marked, blistered future of the earth.

Alessandro keeps climbing. Up! Up! The planet has dissolved to a bauble, the towers of the cities upon the clouds are no longer visible, and still he climbs, now he flies, now he hurtles. And at last he reaches the very last sphere. His body presses against it, and although his mass is no more than that of a trail of smoke, the firmament is just as insubstantial. It gives at first, like a length of cloth, but tautens as he continues his ascent. Alessandro is suddenly aware that there is no atmosphere from which to draw breath. He gasps, sucking at nothing. And then, as he is about to suffocate, pressed against the lining of the universe, there is a ripping sound, the fabric gives way, a new star is seen in the sky above Venice, and he is enveloped by a light so pure that it can only be heard.

# Night and Day You Are the One

Harrah suffered a severe sleep disorder. Like most people, he would lie in bed at night, opening and closing his eyes for several minutes, waiting. As his eyelids grew heavy, however, Harrah would become aware of the pressure of sunlight against them. This happened every night. His eyes would flicker open for a moment, he'd find himself in his darkened room, and then they'd close again. Still the sun pressed against his eyelids, trying to force them open, even after he pulled the blanket over his face. Finally, he'd give up, and this time when he opened his eyes, it would be in an apartment washed with morning daylight, on the side of Manhattan opposite the one in which he had just gone to bed.

Then, of course, he dressed for work. He was employed by two midtown firms. It was an annoyance that the office he went to from his East Side apartment was located out of the way on Seventh Avenue, while the one he had to reach from Columbus Avenue was on Park. The worst aspect of his condition, besides the fatigue, was having to pay rent twice.

Harrah did not consider it to his advantage that this sleep disorder allowed him to maintain relationships with two women at once. It was often a nuisance: two birthdays to recall, two sets of personal endearments, and many complications. Sometimes he'd doze off after lovemaking and immediately find himself in his other apartment with the other woman who, perhaps, after spending the night, had just awakened in a romantic mood. He might then doze off again and return to the apartment where the first woman could either be seeking more attention or have gone into the shower.

Neither Harrah's two groups of friends nor his two families noticed anything unusual about him—he was a remarkably ordinary young man, regardless of where he awoke—and he never discussed his affliction with anyone. Perhaps when the condition first manifested itself he had thought no more than that the second existence was an extremely vivid, if uneventful, dream, but very shortly he lost track of which life was the dream and which was real. Nor could he recall how long he had suffered this disorder, because both selves had vague memories of their lives stretching back into childhood.

Harrah never asked himself which of his apartments was better (the one on the East Side was located on a quieter, better-kept block, but had much less closet space than his Columbus Avenue walk-up), nor which of the two women he preferred. It did not occur to him that he was being unfaithful to either woman.

For years Harrah went on with his everyday life, going to sleep at night in one apartment, immediately waking in the second apartment to attend to his other job (both selves worked in import/export), returning to the second apartment to sleep, and immediately waking again in the first apartment, in the morning following the first night. Perhaps he came to assume that all people suffered this condition, that it was a normal aspect of reality, which was arbitrarily made up of many bizarre phenomena that convinced us of their rightness only by their frequent occurrence. Anyway, this would explain why everyone he knew complained of being tired all the time.

Harrah experienced every day twice, waking twice and sleeping twice. The weather, the ball scores, and the news events that dominated each world usually differed, but not by much, and not in any way that had any real impact on his lives. The television programming in each, however, was identical, and he usually found himself watching the same program twice. Sometimes he'd travel back and forth between both selves in a single day. If, for example, he took a midday nap, he'd immediately wake up in the middle of the night in his other apartment, unable to return to sleep for another fifteen or twenty minutes.

He grew accustomed to these two lives, though he was still occasionally confused—say, in recalling which subway line to take home or, at a movie theater refreshment stand, for which woman he was buying popcorn. Anna preferred it without butter. Also, while he was in one world the detailed features of the second faded in his memory. He could never recall all the digits of his other phone number, and once when he went over from his East Side apartment to Columbus Avenue to look at the other building in which he lived, the block was not as he remembered it, and he couldn't recall the address, and he wasn't sure if it might not have been somewhere on Amsterdam Avenue instead.

After some time Harrah came to ask himself whether it would be appropriate to establish one or the other of his relationships on a more formal footing, or to perhaps secure both relationships. Nothing had really changed in his feelings for the two women, but Harrah thought it might be wrong to remain casual about these affairs for much longer, and that furthermore he was at the right age to marry. He believed he could sense the underlying question of marriage straining each relationship, or at least he imagined that this question *should* be straining each relationship, though neither woman had ever expressed interest in making a long-term commitment. Harrah suspected, without any evidence, that this issue was more likely to be on Anna's mind than on Lillian's, but Harrah could not help attributing the concerns of one woman to the other, even though the women were not similar at all. In fact, to simplify things, he had always assumed that the two relationships were at equal stages of development.

Harrah never spoke to either woman about this issue. For a while it was nearly foremost on his mind, but his jobs were too demanding for him to dwell long on personal matters. He more or less put the question aside, as if by considering it he had resolved it. Now he gave more thought instead to his dual existence, or whatever it was, which raised innumerable questions about the nature of reality, but his spring busy season arrived and he had to shelve this speculation as well. Then one afternoon while passing the shoeshine stand at Grand Central Station on his way home to the East Side, he was struck by a clever idea. A collection of business cards that others had placed to advertise their services covered the wall by the polish and shoelace display. Harrah thumbtacked his own card there.

On his way to work from the West Side the next morning, he returned to the train station. He was surprised—and even disturbed—to find that his card was still there at the shoeshine stand, with his Seventh Avenue office and East Side home telephone numbers. He removed the card. When he reached the office, he called his East Side apartment. There was no answer. He tried several times during the day. That night he went to sleep on the West Side and awakened immediately in the East Side's bright morning sunshine, uncomfortably aware that a ringing telephone had been disturbing him, on and off, for the past several hours.

One evening a few weeks later, he was cooking pasta in his East Side apartment and couldn't find his colander. After searching in vain through his cabinets and even the hall closet, he was forced to drain the water by tipping the pot over the sink and holding the spaghetti back with a fork. Several strands went down the drain and the spaghetti remained wet and became soggy. A few days later the colander turned up—in Harrah's Columbus Avenue apartment, neatly stacked beneath the Columbus Avenue colander. He pulled the two colanders apart and stared at them for a long while, almost afraid to put them down.

Nothing like this had ever happened before. It was an impossibility; of course, this whole business was impossible, but he had come to accept it and the various rules that consistently applied to it. The colander violated those rules, putting everything else in doubt. And although he was at first pleased to have found the colander, he soon realized that he had no way of returning it to his East Side apartment and would have to buy a new one anyway.

Other objects began to misplace themselves and turn up in the other apartment: a tie, a felt-tip pen, an unread book by an Argentine author he had never heard of, a supermarket-bought bag of cookies, and, most maddeningly, the television remote control, which, missing from the East Side, was totally useless on Columbus Avenue. Lillian asked him about the cookies.

"*Pathmark* brand?"

She wrinkled her face in incredulous disgust, an unattractive gesture. Harrah normally stocked this, his East Side refrigerator, with David's Cookies—the shop was only a block away. Because there was no such shop near his place on Columbus, he occasionally bought cookies in the supermarket there. They would sit in his West Side refrigerator for months. He hadn't even missed them.

Harrah shrugged, but perceived that she now harbored certain unflattering suspicions about him and his taste, though there was nothing she said and no change in her manner. Anna left her umbrella one night in his Columbus Avenue apartment and it too turned up on the East Side, in his hall closet. It was an ordinary black umbrella, one that men and women could carry with the same inconspicuousness, but Harrah thought Lil took unusual interest in the article, stopping just short of inquiring how he had obtained it.

One day he had a lunchtime errand down in the financial district, where, as he was stepping from a cab, he saw Anna cross a street. He hurriedly straightened out the tip with the driver. Anna disappeared around the corner of a building. As Harrah rushed to catch her, dodging several pedestrians rushing in exactly the opposite direction, he realized that he had awakened that morning on the East Side—in other words, that it was a Lillian day; he even had a date with her that evening. He stopped and considered the implications. Before this, he had assumed neither woman existed in the other's world. For the first time he felt ashamed about maintaining two romances at once. But perhaps this woman wasn't Anna at all; did Anna really wear her hair like that?

Harrah began hurrying again, but with less confidence, unsure now what he would say to her if it were indeed Anna. He saw the woman at the end of the block, which teemed with office workers and businessmen. She walked briskly, in a gait that Harrah now recognized as characteristically Anna's. As she reached a set of revolving doors, Harrah called her name. The doors swept up and devoured her.

She was gone when he entered the lobby. Harrah told the uniformed man at the desk Anna's name but couldn't recall the name of her firm (which he knew, anyway, was located uptown). Harrah smiled helplessly, apologized for being in the wrong building, and left.

He met Anna for dinner in the evening of the day that began that night when he went to bed.

"I thought I saw you down by Nassau Street," Harrah said. "Was it you?"

"Me? When?"

"Yesterday. Or maybe it was today. Things have been hectic. I'm not sure."

"No, I can't imagine the last time I was that far downtown," Anna said.

"I was sure it was you."

"What was I wearing?"

Harrah couldn't remember. As he tried to summon the details of the encounter from his memory, they evaporated. "I don't know. I called your name, but you didn't turn around."

"How could I? It wasn't me."

Harrah used his lunch break the following day to return downtown, though he knew that finding this woman, this other Anna, was a nearly impossible task: the volume of people on the street was too great, they moved too quickly, most of them were rarely on the same block at the same hour every afternoon. Harrah didn't even know if the woman worked in the building she had entered; like him, she may have been on an errand from another part of the city. Nevertheless, in subsequent wake-on-the-East-Side days, whenever he could get away from the office, he stood on the corner of Pine and Nassau, in the roaring traffic's boom, eating a hot dog, waiting for her to show up.

He never told Anna that he was doing this nor, of course, did he tell Lillian. The hot dog vendor, however, guessed that he was waiting for a woman and winked every time Harrah bought his lunch from him. Meanwhile, as the memory of the chance meeting faded, Harrah began to doubt that it had ever happened. Then one afternoon he saw her, walking jacketless down the street, carrying a white paper deli bag gingerly, as if it contained a cup of coffee or soup that had already spilled and wet the bag.

"Anna!" he called, approaching.

She smiled uncertainly and squinted into the oncoming mass of people, looking for a familiar face. He called her name again and saw that she was puzzled.

"Do I know you?" she said, not quite stopping for him.

"Yes, it's me, Harrah. You don't recognize me?"

She studied him for a moment. Harrah, who looked no different regardless of which apartment he left in the morning, offered her what he thought was his most typical expression.

"No, I don't," she said, shaking her head—exactly how she always shook her head!—and breaking eye contact. She pushed on past him, her head down, evidently dismissing him as another street crazy.

"Anna," he repeated, hurrying to keep up with her against the tide of other pedestrians.

"How do you know my name?" she asked sharply.

Harrah produced his most disarming smile.

"I know all sorts of things about you," he said.

He paused to give an example, such as some funny personal detail about her apartment, or where she had summered as a child, or her favorite movie, but none was at hand. He was aware now that what he had just said was vaguely threatening.

She broke away and surrounded herself with a small group of office workers headed down the block.

Harrah stood there, blinking in the raw sunlight. He watched her as she lost herself in the crowd, just the back of one head among many.

The next morning he called Anna at work.

"Did someone accost you on the street yesterday?" he asked her.

"No. Why?"

This put Harrah at ease. Ever since the previous day, a blister of anxiety had swelled against his heart. Her expression of non-recognition had remained painfully vivid in his memory. They now talked pleasantries for a few minutes. As the conversation approached its conclusion, Harrah's unease returned. He thought he detected an unpleasant edge in her manner. She seemed pre-occupied and eager to get off the phone. He decided to dismiss this as a product of his overactive imagination, though, in fact, no one had ever considered his imagination overactive at all.

"So," he said, "are you doing anything for dinner tonight?"

"Actually, I am."

Harrah was stunned. It was Friday. The question had been only a throat-clearing courtesy. He had assumed they would have dinner together, as they usually did on Friday nights. He was about to ask her what her other plans were, but there was something in her voice, or rather in the silence at the other end of the line, that made him stop.

"All right then," he said, a little coldly.

The two of them now had nothing to say to each other.

At last, she said, "Well, I'll be speaking to you."

"Okay," Harrah said, and then he added abruptly, "Listen, you know those plans you have tonight?"

"Yes."

"Break them."

He was surprised at himself: by the force of his words, by their rudeness, by their desperation. He had somehow given himself away. And the desperation was real and totally inexplicable. His face flushed, and he turned into the wall of his cubicle so that no one else in his office would see him.

She said, "I can't."

Her words fell through the earpiece like two pennies into a puddle.

"There's something I want to talk to you about."

"I'm sorry, I can't."

"Please," he said, his voice faltering.

There was such a long silence that he thought they had been disconnected, but he was afraid to hang up and call back. Then he heard a tentative murmur of assent. That evening at dinner, he proposed; well, he wasn't quite sure what he was proposing, the intervening hours had confused and upset him. He talked in an abstract, metaphorical, almost metaphysical way, he began to stammer, tears rose in his eyes, and then Anna freely wept. She spoke for him, saying that they should live together on a trial basis, with the intention of eventually getting married. Yes, sure, Harrah said, yes, congratulating her as if she had just solved a difficult mathematics problem.

They agreed that her place in the Village was nicer than his on Columbus Avenue. After dinner, they went to her apartment. Both felt amorous, but Harrah gently maneuvered her away from her bed, the place they always made love. She giggled. At his insistence, they made love in the shower, the water blasting his face. Afterwards, she wanted to sleep, but Harrah, saying he was invigorated, suggested they walk to an all-night bagel bakery in downtown Brooklyn.

Anna said he was as romantic now as he had ever been. They returned across the bridge holding hands. The sun was bubbling up through some low-lying clouds in Queens, a new summer morning. Harrah could not recall the last sunrise he had seen.

"I just remembered. I had a dream the other night," she said. "I was running through the streets with something hot in my hands. Then I saw you but I didn't recognize you. It was terrible."

"It was only a dream," he assured her.

"Move in today," she said.

"How?"

"What do you have? Clothes, a few CDs, right? We could make coffee at your place and pack up some things into a taxi. The heavy stuff can come later. You don't know how long I've been waiting for this. I had nearly given up hope."

She hugged him and he kissed her. He had made the happiest decision of his life.

They hailed a taxi and Harrah gave the driver his Columbus Avenue address. The two lovers held hands as the taxi rattled along the empty city streets. Harrah nearly dozed off, but he stopped himself, or believed he had. He shook his body and looked over at Anna, who smiled at him, her eyes bright. Harrah examined every instant of the few minutes they had been in the cab, and each of these instants appeared intact and either the consequence or the precursor of the instants immediately adjacent to them. He hadn't fallen asleep—or perhaps he had, because the cab slowed to a halt at a towering, doorman-attended building on East 86th Street, a building he could hardly recall now, though it was his East Side residence.

Anna showed no sign that she hadn't been there before. In fact, it was Anna, once they entered the elevator, who pushed the button for his floor. With a confidence buoyed by love, Harrah looked forward at last to getting some sleep.

# Among the Bulgarians

A lan returned with his family from a summer in
Bulgaria, and his best friends, Drago and Nadleman,
said, "You didn't get it wet."

They had worked out a code before he left. Alan had
worried that the secret police would read his mail; Drago
and Nadleman figured they would be obliged to show
his postcards to their parents. The code was this: "I went
swimming."

"No."

"No," Drago repeated, mocking outrage. They had
speculated that foreign girls, communist ones especially,
might be less hung up, existing in some kind of parallel,
promiscuous universe.

"If you saw those Bulgarian women . . ."

"No beauties, huh." Looking over his shoulder, Drago
had twisted his face in a smirk that seemed almost
painful.

"*Kuchyeta.*"

That was the plural for the Bulgarian word for dog,
but neither Drago nor Nadleman asked him to translate.
The word just hung there, near the inside roof of the
car. Stabbing at the accelerator, Nadleman lunged onto
Old Country Road, Drago alongside him and Alan in the
backseat. Nadleman had won his license two months
earlier and had already put three thousand miles on his

mother's car. Drago was going for his road test in a week. Alan had missed driver's ed over the summer, of course, and didn't have even a learner's permit. It was a humid afternoon just a few days before school opened.

"The girls have metal caps on their teeth. Gold usually. It'd be like kissing a robot."

Alan immediately regretted his words. The Bulgarians had shown his family enormous warmth. And some of the girls, in fact, had been very nice. At the university in Veliko Turnovo, the capital of medieval Bulgaria, his father had taught American literature to a gaggle of graduate students who believed that they were bewildered by his speech only because they had been taught *English,* while he spoke that notoriously and unreliably slanged dialect, American. Despite his youth, Alan had been invited to all the student parties.

The city was built on the sides of two hills overlooking the Yantra River, which coiled around a promontory occupied by a commanding communist-built monument— four bronze horsemen and a hundred-foot black marble sword thrust into the sky. When not in the student cafeteria or at their parties, or sitting in on his father's classes, Alan had jogged down Veliko Turnovo's terraced cobblestoned streets, the sword almost always in sight through the clotheslines or at the crest of some steps. He squeezed past women in housedresses as they carried laundry through the city's zigzag alleyways. He watched the peasant merchants at the outdoor market playing chess between customers. He shot baskets with wiry local youths, good passers but *short,* who had never heard of Kareem. Alan resisted his mother's blandishments, the museums and old Orthodox churches were left unvisited, but merely the idea of *being* in Bulgaria had fully possessed his consciousness that summer. Not a moment went by in which he could not congratulate, entertain, or console himself with the thought that he was in, of all places, Bulgaria.

"Hey, I have souvenirs for both of you." He pushed two packages over onto the front seat.

"A record," Nadleman guessed, glancing down.

"That's yours. It's by the group, Peace in Our Time. The music's not very good—like the early Bee Gees left on a radiator—but my father's students loved it."

Drago opened his parcel. It contained a gaudy poster illustration of rectangular young men and bright-eyed young women waving red flags and the Bulgarian tricolor. A large portrait of a fiercely sober man with a gallant black mustache hovered above them.

"That's Todor Zhivkov, the party secretary. Underneath it reads, 'Socialism Today Is Yesterday's Communist Tomorrow,' or something like that. I got it off a wall at the school."

As Drago mumbled his thanks, Alan realized that the poster had been a bad choice. It was too big and not interesting enough to hang. Drago would probably shove it into the back of his closet.

"You guys had a good summer without me? Say you didn't."

"It was, like, a tragedy," Drago said. "Like they shot Lennon again."

"You were planning to see Time Machine at the coliseum," Alan said, pleased with himself for remembering.

"Yeah," Drago said. "We planned it, we saw 'em, it's history. Thirty buckaroos."

"Was it worth it?"

Drago made a sound of affirmation without opening his mouth.

Alan was about to ask them if they went anywhere— in the spring they had talked about going camping upstate—but then thought better of it. He himself had gone nearly to the ends of the earth.

"I met a guy who had a Time Machine album," he said. "They're rare. You could get a hundred dollars for one on the black market. And Springsteen, forget it."

Drago slapped a tape into the deck, launching an electric guitar in midnote. The sound ping-ponged around the inside of the car before the rest of the music caught up with it. Alan wondered how many times he had been down this stretch of Old Country Road. Old *Country* Road, he repeated to himself, as if for the first time. Some stranger who had never been to Long Island—say, a Bulgarian—might have expected gently unwinding macadam broken at the shoulders by long grass and wildflowers. He would have found the bright plastic smear of shopping centers and gas stations ironically amusing. To Alan it was, or should have been, the most natural place in the world. He had lived here all his life.

His mother had wanted him to keep a journal in Bulgaria, but Alan had refused. He said he couldn't spare the time. He had seen himself holed up in their dormitory apartment with that ridiculously flowered cloth-bound book she had purchased for him, while outside the room Bulgaria would be happening without him. Furthermore—but he did not tell her this, because he feared these additional reasons might collapse under the weight of argument—recording his experiences would attenuate them. It would destroy his spontaneity, make him self-conscious. And a journal would replace these images and ideas that were pouring into his brain like sunshine through a skylight with whatever language he clumsily chose to describe them, so that years later he would no longer possess the memory, but merely the inexact words.

Unfortunately, now he didn't even have the words. He tried to speak to Drago and Nadleman. The initial sounds of a few sentences—what he had hoped to offer as a series of sharp observations, a brief address, a lecture, a travelogue, a treatise—lay strangled in his throat.

Drago pointed to the right. "A new Friendly's. That wasn't there when you left, was it?"

"No, what did it replace?"

"Good question," Nadleman said and then very mildly chuckled, "Heh, heh." He did it the same way his father did. But then, why shouldn't he?

"Damn," Drago said. "The Beverage Barn?"

"No, here's Beverage Barn coming up."

Alan tried to recall just one of the thousands of times he had been on this stretch of road. He picked at his memory, poking it like something he couldn't see under the car seat.

"Federman's," he announced at last.

It had been a men's clothing store: the Friendly's, surrounded by a larger parking lot, now took up much less room. Alan had never shopped at Federman's, had never wondered who did. It had been impossible to see inside the store from the road, probably because it kept its lights too dim. And—he just recalled—the sign outside had been missing an apostrophe, had never even had one, as if it had been federmans that were for sale. The new Friendly's ice cream parlor, a prefabricated colonial-style building exactly like the one in Syosset, now looked like it had been there forever, or at least since the American Revolution.

"Oh yeah," Drago said. "Federman's."

"I have to tell you," Alan blurted. "Bulgaria was really, but *really* weird."

After a little while, Nadleman said, "Weird, huh?"

Alan was silent for another moment to allow for a rush of recollection: Bulgarians shook their head side to side when they said yes, up and down when they disagreed. For thank you, they often said *merci.* There was only one make of car. When you bought an ice cream cone the vendor proved that he had given you thirty-eight grams by weighing the scoop on an enameled scale begrimed with sour milk. Georgi Dimitrov, the founder of the Bulgarian Communist state, was entombed in a glass case in a Sofia mausoleum. On Vasil Levski Boulevard in Veliko Turnovo, Alan had met two Western engineers, a Nebraskan and a Belgian, who were supervising the construction of a nearby brewery. Employing the shorthand adopted by workers for multinational companies everywhere, they called the city "Viko." Alan and his family took it up as well.

"It's a very closed society," he said.

When Alan had first arrived in Bulgaria, after more than a year of anticipation, he could hardly believe he was there—not so much because of the place's foreignness, but because he had lost faith that the day would ever come. But while he was there, it was hard to believe that America still existed, that his family's home was still standing, that Drago and Nadleman were actually living, breathing, doing something at that instant. And now he had returned home, the trip was over. Well, that too was incredible. He had never expected to journey this far in time. He marveled at the passing of every moment: the fact that he was here, in Nadleman's mother's car, and that this too in another moment would be no more than a memory, a kind of dream as insubstantial as his previous anticipation.

But what was most bizarre about this moment was how real it was, how suddenly alert he was to it. They were driving on the Long Island Expressway now, another segment of Nadleman's lazy late-summer orbit around the planet. The greenness of the grass alongside the road filled Alan's vision, the sans serif lettering of the exit signs softened and modernized the world, he became keenly aware that the intimately familiar place-names they formed—Wantagh, Mineola, Syosset—weren't, after all, English. Drago switched off the tape deck and put on a ball game. Alan couldn't concentrate on the play-by-play. Taking them literally, he was unable to comprehend the announcer's words: "runners on the corners," "the lefthander kicks and deals." The smell of the car's upholstery was pleasantly sour. One of the ashtrays was open, revealing a beige wedge of chewing gum on which was imprinted the contours of the last two teeth that had squeezed it, recognizably molars. A patch of slightly discolored skin, the size of a walnut and the shape of an unknown foreign country, gleamed on the back of Nadleman's neck. It had always been there.

"You know," Drago said, "Nadleman nearly drowned this summer."

Alan was alarmed. "Where?"

Drago snickered. "Lake Solomon."

A pane of glass shattered somewhere. Alan blinked hard against the draft of blood rushing to his face. Donna Solomon was a girl from school.

"Howard?"

"Yeah, we've been going out," Nadleman said judiciously, and a little gruffly. "We went to Montauk a couple of times. Her parents let her stay home when they had to go to California for two weeks."

Alan hadn't known Nadleman and Donna Solomon were even friends. She had been in the film club with Alan, they occasionally walked part of the way home from school together, and once they had run into each other at the Walt Whitman Mall and spent an hour talking in front of A&S. He had even written her a letter from Bulgaria, and it had been answered, without any mention of Nadleman.

Alan watched him. Nadleman was slightly hunched over the wheel, his eyes closely fixed on the road directly ahead. His jowls had thickened almost imperceptibly; perhaps he had even been to a hair stylist. The total effect, however, was that it was not Nadleman driving the car at all, fastidiously sticking his hand out the window to signal turns as if he were still taking his road test, but an exact double. It occurred to Alan that Nadleman's summer had been far more interesting than his.

"That's great," Alan said.

They picked up a bag of cheeseburgers and sodas at the next White Castle, french fries and onion rings at the Jack-in-the-Box on 110, and then stopped at a Carvel on Jericho Turnpike, where they saw a few people from school who had been doing pretty much the same thing. When Bob Finn asked him about his summer, Alan said it had been fine, but no more. Nadleman took them home early: he was going over to Donna's.

At a house near the entrance to their development, two teenage brothers were lazily throwing a baseball between them, one standing at the garage door and the other at the lip of the driveway.

"You see these guys?" Alan said. "They're always here, always having the same catch. The older one stands there, the younger one over there. They never drop the ball and they never throw it away. They've been doing it since they were kids, back and forth, back and forth. I remember when I was small and used to come home late from Cub Scouts, they'd be there. They'll probably be tossing the ball when they're in wheelchairs. And I don't even know their names. They were having that same catch the day I left for Bulgaria, and now I've gone to Bulgaria and come back, and they're still playing catch, and I *still* don't know their names. Nothing's changed."

"Lonny and Peter Hansen," Nadleman said.

"You know them?"

"Peter works in the Rite-Aid by the Syosset Movie Theater. Both of them go to Lutheran."

Alan grunted, overwhelmed by this information. Drago and Nadleman dropped him off.

His mother had been right, of course. He should have kept a journal. Alan kicked at the rug in the foyer as he entered the house. His parents had gone to the beach and the house was as quiet and cool as it must have been while they were in Bulgaria. What a wasted summer, Alan thought; for all that he had gotten out of the trip, he might as well have stayed home and dreamed it. He sat in the living room for a while, staring into the green-gray void within the mind of the sleeping television. He went to his room.

The diary his mother had bought him was there, sitting alone on the desk; she must have just unpacked it. Alan flipped the pages. They were blank, urging their defilement. They even told him what to write, ghostly lines of his own upright, wide-bodied print suddenly shimmering before him, speaking to him. He could hear the cadence of his sentences, nearly make out the words themselves. He wouldn't even need an outline: Bulgaria was laid open to him like a plain seen from a lofty scarp, neatly apportioned into districts of Politics, Culture, Education, Religion, Music, and Sports, each of which he would populate from a wealth of personal observations.

This inspiration lasted no longer than it took him to uncap his pen and position it above the top left-hand corner of the first page. The composition he had seen before him broke up like a cloud in a strong wind, turning as elusive as his vision of his future. The twilight pressed in on his room, dissolving into a gray mist the room's fixtures and furniture, the desk and the journal beneath his fingers, and leaving him astonished by the fundamental strangeness of being home.

# Suit

"How about something in white linen?" twenty-one-year-old Gerard Morton asked his father. "Like what Jack Nicholson wore in *Chinatown*. With a Panama. How's that for making an impression?"

Mr. Morton had been pacing the parquet, too distracted to inspect the goods around him. This was probably the first time in his life that he had ever been uncomfortable in a men's store, something else to hold against his son. He slowly turned toward him, showing wide brown eyes in deep sockets. His gray demeanor registered more pain and anger with every passing day. "Stop it," he said, exhausted. He looked at his watch.

"He's not going to be early, you know. His time is worth too much."

Mr. Morton did not reply, but looked out across the room as if it were an ocean of vast, transparent distances. Gerard, however, knew he was right. Benedict was going to cost his father at least $200,000. "That's college, that's graduate school, and if you ever get married, that's your wedding present," Mr. Morton had told him. The youth, who could not imagine himself going to college or graduate school or getting married any more than he could imagine himself starting for the Knicks, had said, "Good, then we'll be even."

While they were waiting, a smooth-skinned salesman

only a few years older than Gerard offered to take his measurements and led them to a low, carpeted stand parenthesized by two full-length mirrors. He wore a navy blazer and, with equal comfort, a polite deference that managed to avoid any suggestion of servility. It was a trick of adult life so far kept hidden from Gerard, who, in his dealings with authority in a blistering succession of "entry-level" jobs, had sulked so that he wouldn't fawn. As the salesman hunkered with one end of his tape at the bottom of Gerard's jeans and the other held up at his waist, Gerard contemplated passing wind, just to test the guy's reaction.

At that moment—Gerard guessed exactly noon, with bells ringing up and down the eastern time zone— Benedict appeared, grinning like a candidate, his clothes and hair in order as if he had just stepped out of an office in the back of the store, rather than in from the windy, paper-strewn avenue. He enthusiastically clasped their hands, including the salesman in his circle of good fellowship. Mr. Morton beamed. Benedict had wonderful teeth, blue eyes, and short, sandy hair. He also owned a wide, perfectly blank forehead, a pale stretch of skin that might have been more in place elsewhere on his body. Naked, he'd look a bit simple, Gerard thought.

"We want a nice, serious suit for a nice, serious young man," Benedict told the salesman, after shaking his hand. The salesman was too polite to ask why they needed three men to buy one suit. "It should be stylish, but not obviously so. I want him to look comfortable, as if he belongs in it. The message here is quality, without ostentation."

"How about selling me yours?" Gerard asked abruptly. He meant to be derisive, but instead there was an awkward, nearly adolescent edge in his voice. He had to lay back. "So we can get this over with. Or just give it to me as a throw-in."

Although Benedict rarely paid attention to Gerard, he examined his suit now, as if he were indeed considering an offer for it. Gerard wondered how many he owned: he hadn't seen him in this one before, but it was little different from his others. It was elegant, yet professional, completed by wing tips and a silk jacquard tie. A fob that may or may not have terminated in clockwork snaked out of a trouser pocket. Benedict was about thirty-five, but his clothes and accessories gave him the appearance of someone much younger whose confidence, grace, and abilities gave him the appearance of someone much older, about thirty-five.

"It's too smart," Benedict said at last, to Mr. Morton. "We don't want anything this sophisticated. We don't want him to look like some mastermind."

"Absolutely not," Mr. Morton agreed.

"May I suggest gray flannel?" The salesman had a sweet, clear voice. He showed them the way with a grand sweep of his arm. "It's versatile. It shows purpose. Many young men find it rather suitable."

Gerard trailed, trying to keep his face out of the store's mirrored landscape. He had seen enough of himself the day before at the hair stylist, where his long and straight brown hair had been replaced by some blown-dry coiffure that revealed a rash of pimples along the line of his jaw. His stringy mustache had been erased in less than a minute. He thought the haircut highlighted his thick, bony nose and made him look even nastier, but he did not complain, for it was his own carelessness that had delivered him, virtually bound and gagged, into Benedict's hands.

The salesman discovered a light gray single-breasted suit, European styled, he noted, to fit Gerard's angular frame. He proudly showed them the roll of the lapels. Although it was clear that he would never select the first suit he was shown, Benedict rubbed the material between his fingers and said, "Let's see how it fits him."

Gerard obediently donned the jacket. Benedict studied it briefly and scowled, but sent him anyway to a dressing room to try on the trousers. Gerard was surprised when the store's elegance ended at a swinging shuttered door: down a linoleumed corridor was a tiny cubicle with a single loose hook on the wall. The faded carpeting was littered with small papers, staples, and plastic clips. Life. You passed through one facade after another.

He checked the suit's tag, an anemically inked card rectangularly perforated to make it legible to a machine, and it took a few moments for him to pick out the price from among the other numbers on it. Inspection at last revealed the suit cost $999, eliciting a snorted, strained laugh from the youth, who would have guessed three hundred dollars was very expensive. And then a thrilled chill ascended from his belly to his chest, numbing his diaphragm. He missed a breath. The price tag was yet another indication that he was in big, big trouble.

His immediate problems, however, were merely ones

of mortal annoyance. The trousers' unhemmed legs trailed on the floor. To wear them with his shoes— actually, they were his father's old black oxfords; footwear was next on Benedict's agenda—he had to roll them up. Walking through the store, he looked as if he were about to go clamming.

"No, it's too old," Benedict told Gerard's father. "We have to use his youth. Don't get me wrong: it's a nice suit. I'd like you in it. You're a successful businessman. That's the last thing, however, we want it to do for him."

Mr. Morton nodded his head with great seriousness, acknowledging the compliment. Then, disgusted, he reached over and roughly unfastened the bottom button of the jacket, which Gerard had absentmindedly closed while thinking of his shoes. "Goddammit. Act like an adult."

"How's the fit?" the salesman asked him.

"It's sort of like Macy's ballroom."

The salesman didn't respond. After waiting in vain for another taker, Gerard answered on his own: "There isn't any."

No one laughed, the sons of bitches. Macy's didn't have a ballroom. If his father, the guy with the dough, had told the joke, Benedict and the salesman would have been rolling on the floor. In fact, it *was* his father's joke. Gerard had heard it from him ages ago. Anyway, the pants fit all right.

The three other men went off down the aisle, fingering the merchandise and talking about weaves. Gerard followed in languid pursuit, his cuffs coming undone.

His body ached as if, in trying on the suit, he had pulled some muscle.

Benedict was in deep thought, further ennobling his profile, which, Gerard noticed, he always checked from the edge of his eye as he passed a mirror. Only Gerard seemed to notice this breach of earnestness.

Before the Mortons had even hired him, Benedict had insisted on coming to their house, so that, as he said, he could get a better feel for the situation. Upon his arrival—in which he managed to make their doorbell chime with unprecedented portentousness—Gerard's mother and two sisters had emerged from the kitchen and their week-long hysterics in order to fall into complete, reckless love with him, though Gerard could not tell if this was just an effect of Benedict's good looks or in fact his confidence in a house of trembling, loose-boweled men. The women had backed away, afraid they'd give in to their desire to touch him, but Benedict suggested that the entire family be present, that it was a family problem. After a dramatic pause, he added that it was also a family *solution:* the best thing going for Gerard was the fact that he came from a decent, caring home. He was a good boy from a good family, victimized by his own naiveté. Yes, naiveté. Whatever its credibility, the Mortons were grateful for the explanation, for it was the first they had received.

Gerard yawned heavily, hardly able to keep his head up. He could not outrun this avalanche of words and merchandise. An English blazer with gilt buttons was too showy. The twill was stodgy, not believable. The polyester and cotton blend would look just-bought. Benedict decided he wanted collegiate.

In desperation the youth reached into a thicket of tweeds and, with a heavy shove, made a clearing. "How about this?"

"Too preppy," Benedict said after a moment. "People are starting to resent that."

"Well, I like it."

"We're talking retired schoolteachers here, civil servants, minorities. The minorities can be tough. Tweed's not a bad idea, but we want something more SUNY."

"I still like it," Gerard insisted, though now that he had taken a good look at the jacket he realized that he'd rather be hung from the neck than be seen wearing elbow patches. As Benedict moved away, Gerard recalled that he had once applied to the state university at Fredonia—or, rather, that he had begun filling out the application. He had decided halfway through it that he didn't want to attend college after all. "I think it's pretty snazzy."

"No one asked you," Mr. Morton snapped.

"I'm going to be the one wearing the goddam thing."

"And I'm going to be the one paying for it," his father said, his voice down to a searing whisper. Benedict and the salesman were just out of earshot. "You're lucky I don't make you wear what I found you in when I posted bail, you little bastard."

The night Gerard had spent in a holding cell had been a bad one. The arrest had been rough, and his jeans were torn above one knee and he had lost virtually all the buttons to what had been an already frayed workshirt. And, although he did not recall being hit, a large bruise had erupted over his right eye. Worst of all, he had puked on himself, and the cops wouldn't give him anything but a small, unclean towel. By the time morning came, he had forgotten that he had asked them to call his parents. He didn't expect to be rescued; he would spend the rest of his life in jail, in these clothes. "Go ahead," he said now. "See what I care."

Gerard meant it: he saw himself before the judge and jury in rags or, better yet, naked. He would make no defense. The jury would not be shocked. They would understand him. They would take him into their arms, caress and soothe him. He would welcome their judgment, accept any punishment.

"Show me collegiate, but it has to be subtle," Benedict said to the salesman.

"Ralph Lauren has a very fine herringbone."

"I don't see him in anything quite that sporty. It has to be youthful, but classy."

The salesman had gone to a rack of herringbones, but now stopped. He turned toward the three men and tilted his head, like a little bird studying something outside his cage. "Ah," he began. "I'm not exactly sure I can entirely visualize the precise statement we're trying to make."

"Trustworthiness. Naiveté. Innocence," Benedict said.

"Something a middle-class college student would wear," Mr. Morton added.

The salesman made a thoughtful moue.

"I'm charged with selling heroin to an undercover

cop," Gerard explained. "I'm going on trial Monday and they want me to make a good impression."

"I understand," the salesman said brightly. "Very well, come with me."

He led them around a corner of the room to a rack of suits that had escaped their earlier notice. Benedict's eyes lit and he smiled in satisfaction. Mr. Morton murmured his approval. The salesman riffled through the rack, stopped, and said, partly to himself and partly to Gerard, "Let's see. What are you?"

Gerard was about to blurt *guilty*. The salesman, however, answered his own question, suddenly recalling, "Oh yes, that's right. A 38 long."

# The Weather in New York

Jack Latin, retired and divorced, played nine holes of golf, swam a few laps in his backyard pool, and then drove to the airport at West Palm Beach. The temperature was eighty-one degrees. Three hours later he arrived at La Guardia, and freezing rain blew into his face and down his neck. Jack cursed his parents, the only people he still knew in New York. By the time he reached their apartment, two rooms on Eastern Parkway, he had the flu.

"You know, if you moved down to Florida like normal human beings, I wouldn't have to do this every month," Jack told them. He lay on their couch, under two quilts. His mother was setting the table.

"You should see the co-ops they've got fifteen minutes from my house," he went on. "They're beautiful. New appliances, terraces, everything."

"I seen 'em," his mother said, on her way into the kitchen to check on the soup. "They're full of old people."

"Ma, you're eighty-seven. You'd qualify."

"Florida? Hah," his father said, putting aside his newspaper. "It's a hot New Jersey. You go from one damned mall to another. Gas stations, hamburger places—"

"Sun, swimming pools, more sun, golf courses, even more sun."

"Go find a decent bookstore."

"You should take a look at yourselves. You look like ghosts. When was the last time you were down there? Three years ago?"

"It's so boring. All those people could talk about was how much better the weather there is than it is in New York."

"Pop, there's so much to do. You can join clubs, attend lectures, take bus tours—"

"Yeah, kill time."

Meanwhile, the freezing rain had turned to snow. By the following morning there were fourteen inches of it on the ground. The airports were closed and Jack had a high fever. He lay on the couch, watching his mother in the kitchen. Outside the window, which looked out onto the wall of an adjacent building, snowflakes the size of postage stamps fluttered by.

His father, sitting beside him in an armchair, wouldn't allow him to turn on the television except for the news. He refused to play pinochle. He had to finish reading the paper. There was more trouble in Albania.

"Albania? *Albania?* Do me a favor. Look at the weather. What's the temperature in Florida?"

It snowed the remainder of the day. The weather bureau was predicting the heaviest snowfall in twenty years. At about four o'clock one of their neighbors, a young woman, came by with groceries. "I knew you wouldn't be going to the store today."

Jack said, "There's two feet of snow out there. How'd you get through?"

"Oh, it was terrible," she said unconvincingly.

"Have they plowed the streets?"

"Not till May," his father interrupted. "This isn't the Helmsley Palace, it's Brooklyn. Mother's Day or so—that's when we'll see plows. The outer boroughs get squat. I'm going to write another letter."

By the next morning a state of emergency had been declared and the National Guard called out. The highways and roads were closed to all but emergency vehicles. Jack's father piled up a few dozen magazines containing heavily marked articles he thought Jack should read.

Jack's patience, however, was exhausted. How long could he lie on this tiny couch? In fact, the entire apartment was too small. You could barely sit down to eat in the kitchen, or turn around in the bathroom. Ten years earlier he had tried to get his parents into a spacious and airy garden apartment in Douglaston, Queens, but they said, "Douglaston? Who's in Douglaston?"

The question he wanted to ask them now was: Who's in Brooklyn? The people upstairs, the Zucks, who had been living in the building longer than his parents, had packed themselves off to Delray Beach just the week before. Jack didn't know any of his parents' new neighbors, whose impromptu visits carried into the apartment the smells of curry, chili, exotic soaps, and exotic skins. Nowadays you could go from one end of Eastern Parkway to the other and not make a minyan.

Time passed uncertainly, between naps and soup. He was never sure exactly what meal he was eating. Small children, seven- and eight-year-olds reprieved from school, passed through the apartment. They ignored him but listened attentively to his father's lectures about the president's China policy. Jack's mother made *mandelbrot*, but the kids finished it off while he was asleep.

Lou Berger, a member of his golfing foursome, called from Florida. "How's the weather?"

"What? Haven't you heard about the snow?"

Lou chuckled. "Bad, huh?"

"Bad? It's the worst snowfall in New York history. We've already got five feet."

"It's so beautiful here, you wouldn't believe. I'm just wearing a polo shirt, and that's so I don't burn."

"Lou! Did you hear me? *Five* feet—and it's still snowing!"

"And cold too, I bet," Lou said.

All that afternoon Jack lay on the couch. He napped. He listened to the radio. His mother made him more soup. Where'd it come from? Was she making it every day from the same chicken? He napped again.

When he woke, his father was reading the *Times*. "You want a section?"

"No," Jack said. "Wait a minute. Is that today's paper?"

"Herschel Tannenbaum brought it."

Herschel Tannenbaum was a tiny, frail man with a wispy gray goatee and thick glasses. Jack hadn't seen him in years, and hadn't even known he was still alive.

"What do you mean, Herschel Tannenbaum brought it? There isn't a store doing business in the whole of Brooklyn. The roads and highways are all closed. Didn't you hear the radio? Not even fire trucks can get through. The Red Cross has had to open shelters and food-distribution centers. And Herschel brought you a paper?"

"He's a good friend. I know him sixty years. You have good friends like this in Florida?"

"We don't have snow like this in Florida!"

His mother protested as he pulled his trousers on over his pajamas, wrapped himself in a sweater and coat, and stalked out of the apartment. He challenged a similarly bundled man passing on the stairs: "Tell me the truth. How bad is it outside?"

"Pretty bad," the man admitted.

But it was much worse. When he reached the lobby, Jack discovered a mass of snow the height of his chin flush against the door to the building. Its untouched surface stretched as far as he could see through the storm. Eastern Parkway had never before looked so clean.

"It's impossible," he told his father when he returned. "Herschel couldn't have opened the door to the building, much less walk through the snow."

"Herschel is quite a fellow. I give him a lot of credit. Three heart operations and he never complains."

Although he still had a fever that evening, Jack couldn't bear to lie on the couch. He paced the apartment, inspecting the titles of his parents' books and committing to memory every imperfection in the walls. He sighed and tunelessly hummed to himself. His mother warned of a draft, but he stood by the kitchen window for a long time, drumming his fingers against it. The night sky was luminous, filled with snow.

"Our apartment really isn't big enough for three

grown people," his father said with uncharacteristic tact the following morning, while his mother was visiting a neighbor in the building.

"Are you kidding? It isn't big enough for one. You should see some of those places down in Florida. Two bedrooms, a living room, a dining room—I bet you could make yourself a nice paneled study. Wouldn't you like that?"

"Well, I was thinking this way. Why should three people live on top of each other like this? We're not on the Lower East Side anymore. Now, the Zucks left some furniture. I have the keys. Their apartment is very clean. You'd never know they lived there thirty-eight years. You'll be much more comfortable."

"Huh?"

"I'll keep you company. And it's just one flight. You can come down here in your bathrobe."

Jack thought about it. Anything had to be better than the couch. "Well, until they open the airport . . ."

It was true, the Zucks had left a good deal of furniture: an old bed, a sewing table, a working refrigerator, two lamps. Jack opened the radiator and the heat popped and sizzled up through the pipes. There was, however, no TV.

"Good," his father said. "I have some books I want you to read."

"Pop, I'm only staying another day! Maybe two."

"You can start on them."

His father went downstairs for some blankets and linen. Jack glumly sat on the edge of the bed for a while, grew restless, and then started walking back and forth, from one end of the apartment to the other. He imagined he was doing laps in his pool. He picked up a curtain rod and practiced his golf stroke, chipping a crumpled ball of paper into the bathroom. He liked the feel of the curtain rod, it would make a good sand wedge. Retrieving the paper ball, he glanced at the paint-specked medicine cabinet mirror. He was stunned by what he saw.

It was himself, of course, but no one in Florida would have ever recognized him. His eyes had sunk into his head; gray skin hung loosely from his skull. His chest had caved in. He staggered from the bathroom, his temples pounding. Where was his tan?

Finding himself leaning against the window frame, he sadly gazed out onto the street. It was still snowing. And then Jack understood what he must have known in his heart right from the beginning: it was going to snow forever.

# Rope Bridge

Tom and Lucy had been flirting for years. Or had they been? In truth, the affair's history consisted of no more than a few warm glances, hugs of greeting that remained in place a few milliseconds longer than necessary, a lilting ascent in her tone when she spoke to him, an earnestness in his, legs grazing each other in a movie theater. One afternoon when she was getting out of his car, thanking him for a lift, he reached out and gently put his hand on hers. She allowed it to remain there for several moments, and then she was gone. Also, she had once complimented him on a new bathing suit.

"Hey, Dad," said Tom's eight-year-old son, Adam, in the backseat of the car as they sliced along a road cut in the Green Mountains. "They have some crazy music up here."

"Oh yeah, what's that?"

"Falling rock."

His wife, Claire, puffed a tiny laugh through her nose, by way of acknowledgement, and smiled into the sun. Tom had also seen the road sign, but he didn't smile.

"What do you think it sounds like?" Adam asked.

Claire said, "It's probably heavy on the percussion."

"So, Dad, how do you think it sounds?"

"Like your mother said. Lots of percussion."

This was their first trip to New Hampshire since Lucy,

Claire's onetime college roommate, had moved there a few months earlier, to a little hilltop cottage and a design job on a local magazine. They were lost as soon as they left Route 9. Adam demanded that his mother give him the map. She declined and he fell silent. Eventually, Claire put them on the right county road, leading them to the back of their current telephone bill, on which Tom had written Lucy's directions for the rest of the way. They drove along a series of densely wooded passages, over two stone bridges, and then up a steep, inspiring incline. Their last turn was onto a gravel road that kicked and bit at the car's underside before they burst into a sunlit hilltop clearing.

At that same moment Lucy stepped from her odd clapboard house, as radiant and lush as the day. Whole wheat bread and granola, Tom guessed. Waving her arms, she did a little dance of excitement as he parked behind her rust-eaten Nova. The clothes hanger he had twisted around its muffler the previous summer, the day she had joined them on Cape Cod, was still there.

"Welcome to New Hampshire."

Claire said, "Is that where we are?"

"Hey, live free or die. It's on my plates."

The two friends hugged. Tom stepped around the car for the four-hour drive's payoff: a gently applied, moist kiss on his lips, Lucy's slightly parted to suggest the tongue fluttering behind them.

Meanwhile, Adam, who didn't like to be kissed by anyone, not even his grandparents, much less a thirty-two-year-old blonde wearing lipstick, hurried from the car. Leaving the door swung open, he jogged to the edge of the hill. The land fell away at his feet to reveal waves of lesser, tree-covered hills that broke against the horizon, an expanse untouched by human effort. The shadows of a few puffed clouds rode the landscape like aircraft carriers. Adam swallowed a bucket's worth of air and announced, "This is paradise!"

Lucy gave them a tour of the house, whose rooms were stretched along a single axis, making them difficult, she had been warned, to heat in the winter. It was about twenty years old. "The landlord told me the people who built it were from Arizona, and this model had been the home of their dreams. They lasted exactly two weeks after the first frost." She showed them the guest room, the living room, a small den she had outfitted as a studio, and her bedroom. A slight yet evocative depression shaded the center of her bedspread. Tom recognized Lucy's books and things from her apartment in Boston, shuffled and redealt into these strange rooms. A Chinese character print on the wall above her bed, shelves of densely printed college paperbacks, a tiny, unplugged black-and-white television whose face had been scratched during an earlier move—these were clearly the possessions of a single woman, Tom thought. Lucy had broken up nearly a year earlier with a guy she had lived with for five; an easy-going, bantering academic, he had called Tom "Pedro" for no reason at all, but which pleased Tom anyway. Tom wondered what he was doing now.

"Look, this is terrible. You've driven all morning, but now I've got to get to the grocer before he closes. I'm sorry. It's been a gruesome week. I haven't done any shopping. If you like, you can stay here and relax. Or we can all go down and have lunch."

"Sure," Claire said. "I'd like to see the village."

"Are we going to have pizza?" Adam said. "I think I want pizza."

"Pizza?" Tom replied. "What, are you crazy? You can't get pizza in New Hampshire. This is the great outdoors: mountains, woods, streams. They don't eat pizza here."

"What do they eat then?"

"Moose."

"You're lying."

"They do eat moose," Lucy said. "But the restaurant in the village has spaghetti. With regular meat meatballs. You'll like it, I think."

Adam insisted on sitting in the front seat with his father. Tom drove, watching Lucy in his rearview mirror as the two women caught up with each other. The summer had speckled her smooth, frail skin. She looked especially vulnerable, with those pale lips, that round, open face. A vein throbbed across her temple. She saw him looking at her and smiled, holding his stare. Her eyes were not delicate at all.

"What color's the hair around her pussy?" Tom had once asked his wife, before this current infatuation, back when it was just a matter of curiosity. "Is it blonde?"

Claire had laughed.

"Actually, it's pretty dark, reddish. Not as dark as mine, though."

"You mind me asking?"

"I'd rather have you ask me than her."

"Why is it dark?"

"That's how it is. You rarely ever see a truly blonde pussy."

"I never slept with a blonde," Tom murmured, mostly to himself. Claire already knew this; the list of women he had slept with before they were married was a brief one.

"Men usually have darker pubic hair, too," she said.

Tom had nodded, absorbed by a picture of Lucy naked, her vagina covered by dark, reddish hair. He had found it surprisingly easy to imagine.

The restaurant was a bean-sprouts-and-carrot-bread kind of place. They filed into the restaurant, Tom, Lucy, Claire, and Adam. As they were about to take their seats, Adam pushed up ahead past the women and declared, "I'm sitting next to Dad."

During lunch, Tom tried to catch Lucy's eye again. Had that stare in the car meant she was available? On reflection, it may have been less of a stare than a long glance; he needed it repeated for him to be sure. And he too wanted to communicate something, though he wasn't sure what. Meanwhile, his wife was interrogating Lucy about her job: the working conditions, her boss, her prospects for promotion. Tom enjoyed hearing Lucy talk—but not about her job. What kind of woman, Tom wondered about his wife, wasn't interested in her ex-college roommate's sex life? Claire didn't ask Lucy whether she had been dating anyone, so, finally, Tom ventured:

"You don't find it too dull up here?"

"It's quiet," Lucy admitted.

"Is there anything to do?"

"There's movie theaters in Keene, and a playhouse in Peterborough. And they tell me it snows. Next winter I'm going to ski my ass off."

Unbidden, the image of Lucy's small, flat ass rose up in the steam off Tom's omelet.

"Have you met anybody?"

"I knew everyone in town after three fill-ups at the Chevron."

"I meant people our age."

"Sure. There's hardly anyone at the magazine over thirty-five."

Adam asked, "Do you have a boyfriend?"

Heads of the other diners turned at the women's raucous laughter. Adam stared into his plate, trying not to grin, enjoying the response. *This is the wrong lesson*, his father thought: *he'll grow up to be a clown.* Tom forced a chuckle.

Meanwhile, Claire and Lucy went on to discuss Claire's work, and then Lucy asked Tom about his. Tom kept his answers brief. Claire said, "I don't know what's the matter with this guy. Usually you can't shut him up."

She went on to describe in detail the latest progress in Tom's career. Several projects under his control had turned out well; his responsibilities had been broadened. Tom listened to Claire talk about it as if it had happened to someone else, someone he wasn't particularly interested in at the moment—say, Claire's husband.

Lucy said she went to a play to celebrate her birthday.

"What'd you see?" Claire asked.

*Who'd you see it with?* Tom wondered, fully aware of the absurdity of his jealousy. For that's what it was: he slept with his wife every night but couldn't bear the thought that Lucy, on whom he had no claims of romantic affection at all, might be touched by another man.

"It was a new play. I forget the title. It may have been the first time it was produced. Definitely a small-time, small-town production. Listen to what happened. After the play, we went to the bar next to the theater and ordered some drinks."

*We? Who's we? What sex are we?*

"And of course we talked about the play," Lucy continued. "Not too loud, but in normal voices. And I said it needed work. That's all I said, I swear it. Then this guy I never saw before got up, glared at us as if he were about to rip out our lungs, and walked out of the place, slamming the door. 'Oh, by the way,' the bartender told us, 'that was the playwright.'"

Claire said, "You're lucky you didn't say you hated it."

*Us? Who's us?*

If it had been any other woman—even his own widowed mother—Tom would have now bantered, sweetheart, you still haven't answered my boy's question. But Tom knew that he could never ask the question in a way that would camouflage how seriously he sought the answer. Claire might not see through him, but Lucy would.

Tom had long believed that all they needed was a single block of time together, alone and near a bed. The courtship had already been conducted—wordlessly. All that was left was for him to kiss her. But was there any reason for them to be alone? How often in the last ten years had they ever been alone? After all, Lucy was technically Claire's friend. When she told Tom, in one of the many ostensibly casual phone calls he had made to her from his office, that she had finally found a house to rent near Peterborough, he had offered to help her move. "That's sweet," she said, "but I have to do it in the middle of the week, probably Tuesday or Wednesday." "That's okay, I'll take off from work," Tom gushed, envisioning passion among the packing cartons. It was, in fact, famously difficult for Tom to take off from work, requiring negotiated accommodations with his employer and his colleagues. "No, that won't be necessary." "Do you have someone helping you?" he asked. "It's really not that much. I'll be fine," she insisted.

They now returned from the village with groceries. "Okay," Lucy said. "The activity portion of the afternoon has been completed. You can take it easy now."

"I think I'm going to change," Claire said.

"Go ahead." Lucy turned to Adam. "Want to see my horse?"

"You have a horse?"

"It's my landlord's. He keeps it corralled at the other end of the field."

"Can you ride it?"

"No, it's for breeding."

Adam nodded, taking this in gravely.

In the guest room, Tom removed his shirt and watched his wife undress. Marriage and motherhood, Tom and Adam, had hardly touched her body at all.

They had married young; he had courted her with manic persistence—flowers every day for a month, poetry, candlelit dinners—pleased and astounded that he'd make himself ridiculous in the cause of love, perhaps more enamored by his passion than its object. He had finally worn her down, and her body had come to him like a revelation, an exposé of the female form, all bubbling spheres and oblique curves. But now, after the passage of years, it was more like a well-known fact, something repeated so often he could hardly believe it was true. Tom wondered, to his numbing despair, if he would ever want to—really want to—make love to his wife again. He rummaged through his overnighter for another polo shirt.

Claire said, "You know what I just remembered?"

"What?"

"The time you took me rowing on the Schuylkill. You were so romantic. You had a little table, a checkered tablecloth, wine, wine glasses, violin music on the tape deck. It was very sweet."

"But I left the hamper on the pier. Why are you bringing this up now?"

"I don't know. Don't be such a sourpuss. It worked out pretty well."

It had. The useless table kicked aft, they had made love that afternoon on the floor of the boat, the river slapping against the hull. Tom had looked up to see a sculling crew skim the water like an insect less than twenty feet away, each young man indistinguishable from the other, their bodies joined in a single movement.

How could he be so wrong about Claire's mood? In

the car she had hardly talked to him, except to say the most necessary and practical things. How could she be so wrong about *his* mood? She had evidently taken his coldly appraising glances for affection. How could *he* be so wrong about his mood? Now he felt desire uncoiling within him, a mournful tenderness.

"Lucy looks beautiful," Claire said as she went over her makeup. "Really gorgeous."

"Yes," he said noncommittally.

"The country suits her. Fresh air and water every day, a fifty-mile view from her front porch, no traffic . . ."

"It's nice, all right."

"But I think she's lonely."

"Oh, yeah? How can you tell?"

"There's no man in her life." They were standing by the dressing mirror, Claire behind him, Tom still holding his shirt. She kissed his shoulders. *"I'd* be lonely."

"How do you know there's no man?"

"I can tell," Claire said. "Lucy has a certain look about her when she hasn't been laid for a while."

"Yeah, right."

"Don't believe me. You know everything there is to know about women, don't you?"

Tom turned and kissed her.

"Do you get the same look?"

"It puts lines in your face," she said. "That's why I keep several lovers at a time."

When Lucy returned to the house with Adam, Tom watched her closely. Perhaps Claire was right: Tom thought there was an unmistakable tightness around her mouth, and that her motions were abrupt as she prepared drinks for them to take out onto the porch—while Claire's were fluid and nonchalant.

"Dad, you know what I would like? More than anything? A hang glider. You could get one too. We could jump off Lucy's hill and fly back. All we have to do is find some eagles and follow the thermals over the mountains. Mom can drive the car home."

"No, I can't," Claire said. "I'm planning to water-ski back."

Adam was like a very short man, resembling an adult-featured child in a medieval painting—a miniature of his father. He had the same bristly black hair as Tom did, and Claire insisted on the boy wearing it in the same way. "It's cute," she said. "My two men." When Adam spoke, it was with a childishly pitched whine, but also with Tom's inflections, his mannerisms, and occasionally his language. This was what fatherhood had come down to: this compact, mocking figure. There was virtually nothing of Claire in the boy, a fact that didn't seem to disturb her at all.

"You know," Adam said to Lucy, "most people think of the tomato as a vegetable, but it's really a fruit. They thought it was poisonous until 1820, when some guy in New Jersey proved that it wasn't. He showed up on the steps of the local courthouse, pulled one out of his pocket, and took a bite. This really happened. I bet you didn't know that."

"You're a pretty smart kid," Lucy told him.

"Dad says I'm a *pedant.*"

"Have you heard from Josh at all?" Tom asked.

Josh was Lucy's ex-boyfriend. The question startled her. She took a large draw from her drink.

"It just so happens I called him before I left Boston. I hadn't spoken to him in months."

"What'd he say?"

"'Have a nice life.' What was he going to say? It was a dumb conversation. I couldn't explain why I called. It's not like I'm still in love with him. I hadn't even thought of him in a long time, at least not in any serious way. But I met him the week I moved to Boston, and I lived with him most of the time I was in Boston, and he more or less meant Boston to me. So I guess I figured I should say good-bye to him."

"I'm impressed," Claire said. "I wouldn't have done it."

"I see now I can never go back there to live," Lucy said. "The place is just too connected to our history together. To think, the guy ruined a whole city for me. Did I tell you I ran into him on the T, before that? It was a few months after we broke up. His girlfriend was with him. He was his usual shleppy self. Half his shirt collar was sticking out over his jacket, and she was made up like something out of *Dynasty*. Heels, stockings, spandex mini, Giorgio Armani blouse. And tits I'd kill for. I mean serious knockers, out to here."

She straightened her posture and cupped two imaginary breasts well in front of her.

"So we chatted. When they reached their stop, I shook her hand, kissed him on the cheek, and, I don't believe this, nearly fixed his shirt collar. It was pure reflex, I had been doing it for so many years. And then

I realized I would never do it again: that his shirt collar was now foreign territory, like the shirt collars of all other men. How he looked meant nothing to me. I pulled my hand away. They left and I was standing by myself in the middle of the car. I felt like such a fool, like everybody on the train was staring at my tits." She brought her hands against her chest. "Such as they are."

Adam, who was studying a collection of *Ripley's Believe It or Not* cartoons on the steps of the porch, looked up for a moment and then returned to the book.

Claire told a story about a conspicuously buxom woman at work, while Tom pondered the invitation to consider Lucy's breasts. Was she obliquely flirting with him? Not if she was sincere in her belief that her breasts were unattractive. On the other hand, from what he could determine, they were not unattractive at all. He had often seen their shadows, rising up against her shirt. Now, when she touched them, his fingers had tingled.

They played Monopoly that evening. After Tom bought Park Place and Boardwalk, Claire and Lucy were ready to concede defeat. Not Adam, however: he declared that it was not important who won or lost, but that the game be brought to its destined conclusion. Otherwise, it was like not finishing a book or leaving before the end of a movie. With a single low-rent monopoly, two utilities, and an uncanny knack for landing on Free Parking, Adam kept himself solvent for hours. Then at a little past ten he suddenly wound down, burying his chin in his chest like an old man. In exchange for a stay at Tom's hotel on Ventnor Avenue, Claire assumed the task of putting the boy to bed, on a cot in Lucy's studio.

Tom and Lucy were sitting on the floor, their backs against an upholstered chair, their legs in front of them, their shoes off.

"You surprised me when you asked about Josh."

"I'm sorry. It's just that we got along well."

"I know. The two of you were very much alike."

"Can I take it then that I'm your type?"

She smiled and shifted position. Tom's left foot accidentally grazed her instep.

"I may not have a type. I think I've had it with men: their fantasies, their fears, their demands, their housekeeping. Most of them aren't even good company. I'll tell you, Tom, it's a relief taking a break from romance, even from sex. I got tired of the uncertainty, the insecurity. Does he love me? Does he want me? Did he really like it the last time we fucked? Love is such a disappointment."

"Is it?" The word *fucked*, flung out between her top teeth and lower lips, pulled a string in his gut.

"It becomes another measure of age, of the passing of time. Your gums recede, your skin dries out, your love gets overused. It requires maintenance, compromises. Eternal love, my ass—it's the most ephemeral thing in the world. In the end, it diminishes into just another responsibility. Do you know what I mean?"

"Well, I have a wife and kid."

Tom immediately regretted his words. They were disloyal; and, also, he didn't want to remind her of his loyalties.

But Lucy wasn't listening. "What happens as you get older is that the stakes get raised. Everything becomes more important. When you liked somebody when you were young, you went with them to the movies; it was just a matter of preference. Now you have to live with them the rest of your life. And when you're younger you think you know this as a fact of life, but you don't come close to knowing it. So now *this* is what they mean when they call going to work five days a week—week in, week out, no spring break, no three-month summer vacation—a grind. So *this* is what they mean when they complain about getting old. So *this* is what they mean when they complain about death."

Absentmindedly, or so it seemed, Lucy was rubbing her instep against Tom's big toe. Her foot was bare and tawny, while Tom wore white athletic socks. To reach his toe, she had to extend her leg a little further than it had been, slightly tensing her buttocks. Her foot rode up over his toe and down again, back and forth, fitting around it perfectly. It required all Tom's will not to move his foot.

"The first time I took a regular job and got a paycheck I couldn't believe the amount of withholding," he said. "The welfare state suddenly looked a lot less attractive."

"So *this* is what they mean about the loss of love. I had never broken up with anyone I had ever loved before. I had never had the experience of falling out of love. I read the books, I knew all the songs, but I was as unprepared for it as I would have been for a trip to the moon."

Tom didn't reply—perhaps he couldn't have, even if

he wanted to. Lucy's toes were stroking the bony knob at the side of his ankle.

"Is that silence I hear?" Claire asked, returning.

Lucy didn't pull her foot away, but she stopped moving it. Tom kept his in place. It all looked perfectly innocent now. Perhaps it *was* innocent. Perhaps it had never happened.

"No," Lucy said. "I think I hear a bottle of bourbon crying out to be opened."

"Yes, I hear it too," Claire said. "A faint, pitiful sound."

"It's coming from the cupboard above the fridge."

"Let's put it out of its misery."

"Don't forget glasses."

They sipped their drinks in relative silence, Monopoly money strewn around them. A new scenario offered itself: the three of them, in a tangle of love. All they needed was to get a little high, that's all. Lucy lay with her head on the seat of the chair, her bare neck as inviting as a piece of fruit. Claire's head was in Tom's lap, applying a sweet, delicate pressure. As he looked over the rim of his glass, he tried to count every orifice in their bodies and how he would somehow manage to occupy them. A few sips later, Tom became aware of the liquor searing the lining of his stomach.

"Are you okay?" Lucy asked. Her voice was honeyed and warm, so close it seemed inside his clothes.

Unbelievingly, he heard himself say, "No, I think I've had a long enough day. I'm going to bed."

"No!"

"I'm tired."

"Old men," Claire explained, helping him up. He

tottered a little. All he wanted now was to be under the covers with his eyes shut. He didn't want to think about anything for the next eight hours. He didn't want to think about sex, nor about his family, nor especially about himself.

"See you in the morning," he murmured.

Regret, or something, flickered across Lucy's face.

Tom washed and stripped to his shorts, sleepily amazed at the strength of his imagination. He was crazy, no doubt about it. Excess hormones had finally stewed his brain. Claire joined him in bed, innocent of his insanity, unaware of the errant lust that boiled and spat within his head. She grinned seductively and turned off the lamp. "I'm drunk," she announced.

At the moment he kissed his wife's lips, Tom thought of Lucy, and how her body would feel under him and how her mouth would taste. Claire fell back into her pillow. As Tom again kissed her, nuzzling the short hair at the back of her neck, he realized she was asleep. He pressed his lips against a shoulder blade. She can't drink either, he recalled.

A great surge of affection swept away his sleepiness. With his body spooned around Claire's, his arms wrapped around her chest, he was frustrated that they could not be even closer. He squeezed her. She didn't wake; she didn't feel him against her at all.

Meanwhile, Lucy was in the next room, probably asleep, possibly not, possibly sensitive to his nearness. He pursed his lips again and sent Lucy a telepathic kiss that moistened the inside of an ear, and then another at the hollow where her neck turned into her right shoulder.

*Lucy, are you awake?* Was she? *What are you wearing?*
Probably gym shorts and a T-shirt. Or nothing at all, her
body stretched naked across the bed, hugging a blanket
or pillow. His antennae bristled, awaiting a reply.

How passionate was he? Enough to cheat on his
wife? He never had. Was that normal? In literature and
in films, illicit love was typical. Yet in real life he didn't
know a single friend capable of adultery. Tom himself
had descried opportunity among the women with whom
he worked, several opportunities that any protagonist in
fiction would have taken, and he had passed them up,
to his immediate sorrow and lasting relief. Was he less of
a man because of this—or, more seriously (because the
question of manhood was trite)—was he less a man of
passion? Sex was the least important aspect of this.
What was at stake was a matter of character.

Tom stared at the wall that separated him from Lucy.
He imagined her on the other side of it, staring back at
the wall. And then Tom slept, to wake again, every few
minutes, to think how it was that he wanted her in the
worst possible way, and then to sleep again.

An hour before dawn Tom woke with a thump, his blad-
der full and his mouth sour. For a moment, he could not
remember where he was. When he did, he grimaced.
Desire returned to him like a toothache—specifically, an
unfilled cavity. He stepped from the bed, tapped the chill
wood floor for his slippers, and recalled that he had left
them home.

Padding down the hallway to the toilet, he passed the

open door of the studio, where Adam slept in red bottoms and a blue T-shirt, an outfit that Claire had bought him during his Superman phase, when he regularly wore a red cape in the street. Now, thank Krypton, it had been relegated to sleepwear. The boy slept exactly as his father did, with his head buried in his pillow.

Lucy's door was just across from the bathroom. It was only slightly ajar, and Tom couldn't see anything inside the room, not in his single furtive glance into the darkness. He closed the bathroom door and urinated by the shine of a gibbous moon behind the curtain.

The relief of one discomfort aggravated the other. From the bathroom he went to the kitchen. He slitted his eyes against the refrigerator light and found a jar of cranapple juice. He poured a few swallows into a plastic cup that had been drying on the rack by the sink, drank it, lightly rinsed the cup, and returned the jar. As he stepped from the kitchen, as silent as a ghost, another specter blocked his way.

It was Lucy in a long peach nightgown, her face awakened by surprise. She stared at him in alarm for a moment, as if she had forgotten other people were sharing the house with her that night. Wrapping her arms around her upper body, she stepped back.

Tom was just as startled.

"I had to use the toilet," he whispered. "And I was thirsty."

She nodded in confusion and shuffled past him into the bathroom.

He asked, "Do you want something to drink?"

"All right," she mumbled, closing the door.

Tom returned to the kitchen. When he opened the refrigerator again, he didn't have the least idea of what he was looking for, and once he recalled the juice, he couldn't find it. Within the minute that he left the kitchen, met Lucy, and then returned to it, every item in the refrigerator had been replaced by inedible artifacts from another planet. His mind was blanker than it had been in the deepest abyss of sleep. He stared into the refrigerator light for what seemed like the rest of the morning until, jarred alert by the cheer of the flushing toilet, he finally found the juice. He poured it into the same cup he had used.

Lucy was hanging back inside the shadow of her bedroom doorway. With one arm around her waist, as if she were cold, she reached for the cup. Her arm was bare— a mile of naked skin. Her motion swelled her breasts against the top of the gown. She tasted the juice and offered him a modest smile, the moonlight shimmering on her lips.

There was no good reason for Tom to remain standing there. In fact, he wanted to squeeze past her and return to his room, to flee and hide under the covers. Yet he couldn't move. In better light, he thought, he would see right through her gown.

She finished the glass and absentmindedly handed it back to him. Her mouth framed her thanks. Holding her eyes, he took a step toward the cup, and then he took another—it was like stepping onto a rope bridge—and, quickly closing the last few inches between their faces, he kissed her.

It wasn't like kissing her hello. Her mouth remained clenched and she pulled away.

Fragments of nervous jokes flashed through Tom's mind, none good enough to laugh this off. He was aware of his own near-nakedness: not only that he was wearing shorts, but that he had irrevocably exposed himself. Lucy's eyes were open wide now, taking everything in; their wideness revealed a voluptuous beauty that he had never before noticed. He was also aware of the detritus of sleep encrusted around their rims, making her appear nearly as exposed as himself.

He kissed her again, for want of anything else, and again Lucy's lips held out. The third time he kissed them, they opened just a little. He tasted cranapple. With the cup still in his hand, he put his arms around her and felt her lift up toward him. *Live free or die.*

Neither dared break the embrace until they were in the door of the bedroom. He shut it. He put his arms around her again, and her nightgown collapsed into a pile around her ankles. Still standing, he pulled off his shorts. For a moment both were too shy to look at anything but each other's faces. Lucy's still showed fright, and more than a little wonder at what she was getting into. What *was* she getting into? What did this mean? Tom himself didn't know. Making love to a woman who was not his wife—this was a gerund phrase from another language. He ran his eyes over her body, vowing to remember this forever: the pale luminescence of her skin, the curve at her hips, the buoyancy of her breasts. The hair around her vagina was indeed dark, but how dark was impossible to tell in this light.

As he tasted Lucy's skin—salty and a little sourish—
she shuddered. She didn't speak. Sprawled back on her
bed, she bit down on the edge of a pillow, grinning
tightly and without humor. Her hips rose to meet him
with a predatory urgency he found shocking. So: every
gesture, every glare, every comment that he had thought
part of a casual and ambiguous flirtation had, in fact,
been a demand. Their lovemaking (Tom feared) disturbed the house's quiet like a skater on a lake of thin-
ning ice, every shifting of their weight breaking distant
microscopic crystals. There was a loose screw in the bed-
frame that rattled twice in every stroke, one rattle at a
slightly shallower resonance than the other. The bed-
springs, too, had a small, irregular noise, as did the friction of their bodies against each other and against the
sheets. Tom even thought he heard the joints between
their bones cracking. Lucy moved under him hard,
needing him much more than he could ever have been
prepared for. Her extravagant moistness, the strength
with which her muscles pulled at him—it was as if he
had caught himself in some dangerous mechanical device. So *this* is what she meant by *fucking*.

"Dad? Dad?" Then more insistently: *"Dad!"*

It was Adam, right outside the door. Tom pulled out
of Lucy so quickly she gasped. She grabbed his hips, trying to draw him back in. He tore from her hands and
found his shorts.

*"Dad?"*

Tom opened the door just a crack. Adam was standing there, his cape twisted around to the front of his
shirt. His eyes were unfocused, like a sleepwalker's.

"Dad," he said.

"Shhh. What?" Tom stepped from the room, shutting the door behind him.

"If there was a war between the Star Trek Federation and the Star Wars Empire, who do you think would win?"

The boy didn't wait for a reply, but stumbled away down the hall, past the studio.

"Whoa," Tom whispered, catching up and turning him around. "Your mother's sleeping."

"So who do you think would win?"

"The Empire," Tom said. "They have the Death Star technology. Not to mention the Dark Side of the Force."

They had gone over this ground just a few days earlier; Adam had come up with the answer himself. His hand pressed against the boy's back, Tom now led him to the studio. As if in a trance, Adam climbed into the cot, wrapped himself in his blanket, and closed his eyes. Tom stood by the bed and watched him for several minutes. Adam didn't move at all in this time; he hardly breathed. Tom waited for his own breathing to slow, and for his pulse to cease thumping in his ears. He returned to his bedroom, where his wife lay in the same position in which he had left her.

Tom's spinal column grew several inches in the next few hours. In the morning it was ramming against the top of his head, squeezing the contents of his brain against his eyeballs and eardrums. Brilliant sunlight savagely broke into the bedroom. Birds outside the window screamed and wailed, tearing the air like rusty razor blades. When he and Claire arrived in the kitchen, there was a glass of cranapple juice at every place setting around the table.

"The batter's mixed," Lucy said, handing him a spatula. "The rest is up to you."

She smiled at him, but the smile was neither complicitous nor flirtatious, nor annoyed, nor wrathful, nor embarrassed, nor perplexed. Against all odds, it was just a smile. She stepped away to bring Claire a cup of coffee. Tom vaguely recalled boasting about his skills as a pancake turner. It had been in another life, in a galaxy far away and long ago. He stood for a moment at the screen door. Adam was already outside with his net, looking for butterflies at the edge of the hill.

"Dad, I almost caught one!"

Now, what did *that* mean? Tom approached the bowl and stared into it. Lucy was telling Claire an apparently amusing story about a fender bender she had suffered in Nashua; Tom listened intently to her words for some hidden message directed either to Claire or himself. He listened further for all the particular sounds of the country: the drumming of their claws on the bark as two squirrels chased each other around the trunk of a maple, his son stamping through the high grass, the whir of some fantastic insect, the tentative creaks in the structure of his life before it fell down around him. His head felt like it had not yet adjusted to the altitude.

Claire said, "So, you've studied the problem. Now how about greasing the skillet?"

Tom burned the butter. He ran the bottom of the pan under water to cool it, greased the pan again, and burned it again. Sighing theatrically, his wife left the room to dry her hair.

He was alone with Lucy. She read the paper, her back to him. Was she aware they were alone, that he was watching the back of her bare neck, trembling? She turned and raised her head toward him, her face lit in the sun like a new penny. Adam burst through the door.

"I really need help," he said. "You don't expect me to catch butterflies by myself, do you? I'm only eight."

"After breakfast," Tom said.

"Are you making pancakes? Can I watch?"

He shrugged. "If you like."

Tom poured the batter and stood by the range, Adam counting the bubbles rising through each pancake. When the boy, aware that his father was staring at him, turned up his eyes, Tom looked away. Lucy said, in a voice husky with promise, "Why don't you have a cup of coffee?"

"Sure."

"I'll get it for you, Dad."

It was as if it had never happened, as if it were some terrific dream, a dream of her breasts and her tart tongue. Suddenly, the dream's significance thundered at him, and in the lightning flash that preceded it he saw himself, Claire, and Adam, and Lucy too, a year hence— love sundered, friendship sundered, all of them cast into the abyss, the world's sum of loneliness increased— a year now held off. But here it was morning, and their lives were intact. In his mind, the shadows of the darkened house were blown into clouds of neural fog, disassembling and reassembling pieces of his memory. He couldn't recall Lucy's body. Here in the daylit kitchen, it was hard to believe he had ever made a pass at her. Except for one thing: this morning when he woke, his dick had been wet.

They finished breakfast late. A walk along a trail near Lucy's house occupied the remainder of the day. Tom and Lucy were never alone. Claire was there, of course, close to Tom, a hand around his waist or in the back pocket of his jeans and, once or twice, arm in arm with Lucy. The few times she was out of sight, Adam stayed near, hectoring them about the internet, Power Rangers, and Esperanto. Whenever Tom tried to catch Lucy's eye, she was facing away from him, or looking beyond him; when he tried to avoid her gaze—as the implications of what they had done the night before once more assailed him—he found her directly across from him, on the edge, it seemed, of saying something.

The afternoon deepened and their return home approached in a rush. They packed their bags and loaded the car, including four jam jars of "unusual specimens" that Adam had discovered on their walk. The sky blued and thickened, hushing the valley below Lucy's house. Birds slept, or perhaps were just caught on the wing between songs. The earth had stopped for the moment Tom stood on the hill, his overnighter in his hand.

"I don't want to go," he blurted.

"Stay," Lucy said lightly.

Tom turned to her. A length of hair blew across her impassive face. There was no sign that she had just spoken. Tom watched the strand dangle as if he might learn something from its motions.

"We'd love to," Claire said, "but Tom doesn't have any personal days left."

"I feel that if I go, I'll never be able to come back."

Claire smiled. "I'm sure Lucy will invite us again."

Lucy didn't say anything to this.

"It won't be this weekend," Tom murmured. "It'll be another weekend."

"Uh-huh. That's how time works," Claire said. She was about to grin, but stopped, glimpsing something unsettling in his expression.

"Are we going or what?" Adam called from the car.

Lucy and Claire kissed, brushing each other's cheeks, and Claire buckled herself into her seat. Lucy walked around the front to the driver's side. Tom stood there, caught between the open door and the car, clutching his keys. He smiled tentatively. With the door between them, their heads hidden from the occupants of the car, she kissed him directly on the mouth. It was with as much affection as she had kissed him upon his arrival, but no more. Or did Tom see in her eyes something wistful, or angry, or sad? He thought he did, he was sure of it—but perhaps he was wrong. Before he could kiss her again, she had stepped back.

Claire and Adam waved good-bye as Tom pulled the car away. He looked at Lucy in the rearview mirror, standing at the edge of the clearing. She waved once and began the walk back alone to the house. Her head was bent low and her hands were in her pockets. She seemed to be studying the ground. The setting sun flashed in the mirror, obliterating the scene, and when the image cleared, she was gone. Neither Tom, Claire, nor Adam said anything as they coasted down the hill, the car in neutral, riding the thermals back home. Tom watched his son, sitting directly behind him and Claire, his expression subdued, perhaps reflective. Or perhaps he was just a little sleepy. Tom made a mental note: he'd have to ask him what happened. Say, in about forty or fifty years.

# Invisible Malls

*Kublai Khan does not necessarily believe everything Marco Polo says when he describes the indoor shopping malls visited in his travels around the empire, but he listens to the young Venetian with greater attention than he has shown any other messenger or explorer. He has already heard Marco's tales of invisible cities, of Diomira and Despina, of Zirma and Isaura, calvinoed metropolises built from memory and desire, and he waits for further intelligence. The aged emperor has reached the melancholy moment in his life in which he needs to comprehend his conquests, when the illuminated maps hand-drawn in rare inks and paints by Tartary's greatest cartographers only frustrate him. As beautiful as these maps are, they are unable to show the borders of his vast territory, and they are also very difficult to fold. The Khan has no use for the blunt, irrelevant reports of functionaries, emissaries, generals, and spies. Only in Marco Polo's account is the Khan able to understand what his will has accomplished.*

## Indoor Shopping Malls and Memory 1

Leaving there and proceeding for three days toward the east, you reach Monica, an indoor shopping mall entirely occupied by the past. Crowding one boutique after another are Mickey Mouse watches and souvenir ashtrays from the 1939 New York World's Fair, stretched Coke bottles, incense candles and Day Glo posters, smile decals and fake gas lamps, pet rocks and electronic pet birds. Monica's merchants have already placed orders for merchandise nearly obsolete but not yet in fashion. The mall has structural defects and a short lease on the land, but the merchants know they will stay in business forever. They envy their customers, who believe they were happy when they owned what the merchants own now.

## Indoor Shopping Malls and Desire 1

In the shops of Alice, you can buy philosophers' stones, golden fleeces, holy grails, concubines of absolute beauty and passion, books that answer the questions posed by wise men and children, and elixirs that deliver eternal life. Each of these items, however, is priced at slightly more than you think it's worth, plus sales tax. After you've left without making a purchase, you feel the difference between what you want to pay and what the goods cost as a little hole burning into the lining of your stomach. You realize that the item is worth more than you thought. You return to the store but find the price has been raised to a new figure that is really un-reasonable. Annoyed, you again leave empty-handed, reconsider and return, find the price has been raised again, leave once more, and so on, forever.

## Indoor Shopping Malls and Sleep 1

The items in Larissa's shops relate to the many aspects of sleep. These include sheets and bedspreads, of course, and pillows as soft as clouds, comforters of per-fect comfort, gossamer negligees weaved by genetically engineered Peruvian spiders, as well as bedside tables, bedside lamps and bedside books that, in the disjointedness of their narratives and the vagueness of their metaphors, are written to ease the transition from wakefulness. Across the way, a small shop sells a single line of alarm clocks that are individually calibrated in order to rouse each customer with the most urgency that can be obtained with the least amount of discomfort. The other shops that line Larissa's softly lit corridors supply the foreshortened hours between night and dawn: for example, notebooks whose pages have been chemically treated to better capture the evaporating details of your dreams. These shops also sell the committed sleeper devices to intensify the vividness of his dreams, others to minimize the same dreams, computer software that program dreams, and mass-produced dream rentals. Here are scales that measure the weight of your nightmares and calipers to measure their width.

## Indoor Shopping Malls and Desire 2

There is no parking lot at Carolyn. Would-be shoppers drive around it for hours, looking for a place to leave their cars. Bewitched by the illusion of a parking space glimpsed in a rearview mirror, or through the windows of intervening vehicles, or in some parallel universe visible only from the corner of the eye, some drivers abruptly back up, turn, accelerate without warning, or attempt to squeeze between other cars. There are numerous collisions. Most of the drivers, however, allow themselves to be entertained by their car radios, snack on whatever provisions they have brought with them, and then return home. If they voice any complaint, it is only with the amount of traffic they have encountered.

## Indoor Shopping Malls and the Sky 1

Like other indoor shopping malls, Rachel is roofed, its internal climate regulated by hidden machinery. Daylight is allowed into the building only through its doors. Yet before the shopper can focus his eyes on the racks and display windows ahead of him, they are directed upwards to a fantastic apparition. Where in other malls are nondescript ceilings, Rachel's master engineers have installed an intricate mechanism of lamps, gears, pulleys, cams, flywheels, springs, and weights that approximate the silent churnings of the universe. Clockwork drives a mammoth lamp, the mall's sun, across a painted sky, and then raises a lesser lamp, a manic face etched in its glass, the mall's moon. The mechanism's motion is accelerated to encompass a full day, from sunrise to sunrise, during the mall's business hours. Planets move forward and then in retrograde, and hundreds of thousands of lights suspended by wires wheel above our heads. As a service to their customers, Rachel's merchants have also arranged to make visible to the unaided eye what God cannot: galaxies, nebulae, clusters, quasars, pulsars, novae, planetary discs, meteor swarms, and interstellar dust clouds. The shopper need not emulate the astronomer's patient attendance to the heavens. Rare and spectacular celestial events, such as eclipses, occultations, conjunctions, and transits are scheduled to appear at least once every day.

## Indoor Shopping Malls and Desire 3

From the moment you step into Sophie, you are overcome by aromas sweet, pungent, sour, and meaty. Sophie is exclusively a food court, offering not only ice cream, pizza, popcorn, and tacos, but also manna, loquats, and ambrosia, all of it deep-fried. Strolling down the concourse with a sixteen ounce cup of immortality-conferring amrita in one hand and a hot dog in the other, you pass strangers who are drinking kvass or goat's milk, or nibbling Uzbek plov or shark nuggets, and, enveloped by the grease-laden steam wafting over the formica counters, you wonder what you will eat next. But food is the least of your desires. Where are the public restrooms?

## Indoor Shopping Malls and Time 1

Not a single watch or clock is sold in Lucy. Indeed, visitors are asked to leave their timepieces at the coat check, lest the relentless ticking of their mechanisms fracture the delicate goods within, as it does outside the mall. Lucy is devoted to time in its deepest, sourish essence and diverse manifestations: lost time, time made, time that stands still, daylight savings time. Aware that their product is a sensory illusion caused by physical motion, the merchants run the entire mall on a railroad track around the parking lot. The shopper is invited to stand still and allow the eons to wash over him like an ocean on its way to becoming a desert. For clients who are habitually late for their appointments and trysts, Lucy's retailers sell packets of time purchased wholesale from those who are always punctual or even early. The former conventionally swindle the latter; Lucy imposes an orderly and just economy upon them.

## Indoor Shopping Malls and Memory 2

Emma is so up-market that its boutiques are named for designers that you have never heard of; nor are you allowed to hear of them. If you do learn the names of these designers, Emma's security commandos abduct you to a secret location within a remote discount store and chemically induce memory loss. If the commando team fails (induced memory loss is still a developing field), the shop goes out of business and is replaced by a store dedicated to an even more exclusive designer, selling clothes at prices too high to be pronounced by the human voice.

## Indoor Shopping Malls and the Dead 1

In malls from Paramus to Zanzibar, adolescents wash down every promenade, crowd every aisle, besiege every register, and monopolize every video game. A population in pained transition, its records, jeans, toys, and bedroom decor are also in transition, coveted one day and discarded the next. The exception to this state of affairs is Gloria, an indoor shopping mall located in a subterranean fissure. It is patronized exclusively by the dead, who shop without hurrying, who can wait for closeout sales, and who buy goods to last forever.

*Marco Polo does not know if the Great Khan is sleeping or awake: his eyes are closed and his breathing is slowed, but the long lines of his face are drawn into a contemplative frown. The emperor is, in fact, awake, considering indoor shopping malls so far unmentioned, in Manhasset and Shaker Heights, in Boca Raton and Bel Air. He is thinking of the Galleried legions, and of big old GUM staring down at the tsars. "So this is my empire," Kublai Kahn murmurs. "These are the subjects who send me their tributes and raise my armies, who follow my laws and who whisper my name to either threaten or calm their children. These are the people whose poets address their songs to me." "No, sire," Marco Polo replies. "The malls are only home to goods. The promenades are emptied, the shutters are drawn, the fountains are stilled, and the coin purses are fastened shut with the fall of dusk, except on Wednesdays, when they are open to nine. The shoppers return to their residences, where they are alone as if in death, subject to nothing, part of nothing. Your empire is quiet halls and shelves, locked display cases and bare cash drawers." As night rushes into his palace's luxuriant gardens, the emperor cannot tell if the traveler smiles or weeps. But he knows now, at least, why Marco Polo has so many charge cards.*

# No Grace on the Road

I

The peasant couple first thought we were doctors. Their infant son was ill. His grandfather had been sent by bicycle the day before to the nearest telephone, which was in the post office at Pat'in, about ten strenuous kilometers north, in order to summon an army physician from Sempril. At the time of our arrival, in the midst of a storm that left us at their door gasping for air, the family was engaged in a tense and solemn vigil.

It was with great difficulty that I made them understand that neither of us was a doctor. I did not even try to explain that I was an economist. There is no word for economist indigenous to our language. In the capital we usually employed the French cognate, though the government of the day had officially replaced it with a newly coined one derived from the native expression "he who tallies cattle." It was an especially inappropriate term for use in a country whose dairy industry had declined to the position where it could no longer supply milk even to that part of the population that was under five years of age.

"Can you not do something?" the child's father asked.

"I just told you. I'm not a doctor."

"I do not understand," he said, perhaps accusingly,

as if he were claiming that my slight, persistent accent somehow made me unintelligible.

"Our jeep broke down. It's about a kilometer down the road," I told him again. I wanted to step away from the infant's pallet: I was unsure of the age at which children began to understand speech. "We're traveling to the capital from Queling."

"The army sent you from Queling?"

"The army didn't send us. I'm on leave."

The man stared at me. He still didn't believe that we had not come in response to the grandfather's summons.

"But what were you doing at Queling?"

Annoyed at his thickheadedness and his impertinence, I assumed a military posture, looking just a little bit past him, and identified myself: I was a reserve officer, Sublieutenant Palin Ni Lap, under the direct command of Major General Ti of the Third Patriotic Division.

I pronounced each word carefully, sure that at least one would make an impression on the couple. But none did. They turned and, still seeking a doctor, looked to the completely alien figure warming itself by the small peat fire.

I explained: "This is my wife Leslie. She is from Westchester, U.S.A."

Hearing her name spoken, my wife offered the couple a smile that, although diminished in recognition of the child's condition, nevertheless consisted of more teeth than could be counted among the peasants' communal property. She was sitting on an old Coca-Cola crate partitioned to hold deposit bottles, a relic from the days when empties were shipped to a bottling plant outside

Bangkok, making a small profit for our fledgling trucking industry and producing a certain amount of revenue for our Roads and Customs Department. Indeed, empty Coke bottles were once a major export item. Now no-deposit cans lay spent meters from the spot where they had given up the last of their juices. Our trucking industry was moribund, all but the most marginal concerns bought up by Indian entrepreneurs who had the capital, the contracts, and the volume to operate them competitively. Of course, the officials of the Coca-Cola Company eluded reproach; in fact, they could point out that some of the savings of using cans had been passed on to the consumer, making the soft drink available to a greater number of my countrymen than ever before. It was just something that came to mind whenever I saw an empty Coca-Cola crate. The Hotel Progress in the capital used two of them, installed behind the check-in counter, to hold guests' post and keys.

Three small children stood across from my wife, absolutely transfixed by the extravagant curls of her light brown hair. Sitting on a makeshift couch, an elderly woman, an amorphous mass of distended skin, stared at her, turned away, cackled obscenely, and turned back to stare.

The peasant glanced at his young wife, trying to gauge how well she understood the gravity of the situation. Her head was bowed.

"You are from the capital?"

"Yes."

This had an even greater effect on him than the fact that Leslie was an American or that my family's name

was one of the most famous in the country. My grandfather had owned the largest plantation in the adjacent
province. My uncle was the publisher of the country's
single daily newspaper (though the government was
technically its sole owner, in trust for the people, only
eighteen percent of whom were literate). My father,
a former deputy ambassador to the United Nations, was
now Minister of Posts and Telegraphs. But what mattered
to the peasant was that I was from the capital, a city.

"This is our certified residence," he stammered.

"Fine."

"I have my papers."

He took a painful step toward his wife, revealing that
he was partially disabled. The fronts of his torn cloth
shoes stared at each other. His back arched to the right
of his hips. Such misfortune was not unusual in my
country; if it was not the legacy of childhood rickets,
then it was the outcome of a losing confrontation with
some sort of imported machine. For a non-industrial
nation, we suffered a good many industrial accidents.
There wasn't a collective farm in the country that hadn't
made an offering of at least two limbs to its combine.

"We don't want your papers. We ask only for a place
to spend the night."

"Get them," the peasant told his wife.

"I told you. I don't need to see anything."

A sudden fit of strangled cries coming from the object
on the pallet interrupted us.

"That child sounds awful," Leslie said in English.

The children gasped, surprised that she could speak.
Of course, she was completely unintelligible to them, but

her voluptuous voice, plumped and edged by her native region, nasaled just enough to identify the suburb with the city that gave it any meaning at all, was as strange and wonderful as her curls, and as eerie as the cries of the sick child.

"They know it," I replied.

The peasant repeated his order to his wife, discomfited that words secret to him were being exchanged in his home. She did as she was told and also removed a bundle of rags from a large carton.

"Dry yourself and change into these," she said to Leslie and pointed to a screen at the other end of the room.

Leslie knew only a few phrases of my obscure native language, and she knew them rather badly. Nevertheless, she spoke the language better than all but perhaps thirty other Westerners in the world, and she understood the woman's invitation. She ducked behind the screen, which in fact was a genuine, if somewhat battered, home movie screen salvaged from God knows what dump, mounted on a low tripod as if the peasants intended to show us slides from their vacation on the Côte d'Azur as soon as electrification reached this part of the province.

No one offered me a change of clothes, nor did I expect any. I resigned myself to examining the family's official documents, which were bound by an old and frayed length of, what? Dental floss? This dilapidated shed was indeed their certified residence. They had each been born in this district. He was twenty-four and she was twenty-two. Krik and Sana. He had served nearly two years in the army, but only in the "reconstruction corps" of conscript workers, and had probably not left the province once in his life. His injury was recent: he owned an "heroic sacrifice" early discharge. The old hag, age forty-six, was Sana's mother. The couple had four children ranging in age from five months to seven years. Miraculously, everyone was properly vaccinated or, almost as miraculously, given their poverty, immobility, and unsophistication, they had managed to get their vaccination papers forged.

And although I had never met this family before, there was certain, even more intimate information about it in my possession. I knew its annual income, its average daily intake of protein and carbohydrates, and its members' life expectancies. In air-conditioned offices in New York, Paris, and Geneva, these profound truths were objects of commerce.

I returned the papers without comment and performed the intricate ritual of asking for shelter, and Krik went through the intricate ritual of agreeing to provide it. My military rank alone would have obliged his co-operation, as would have my social position and, of course, my gun, but this formal ceremony—whose florid excesses would have appalled Leslie had she understood what we were saying—provided a means of expressing dire need and mandatory hospitality without awkwardness, unmanly deference, or ambiguity. For me to rend my people's language into English literally would be to indeed rend it; it would make the language appear ludicrous, its forms affectatious and its syntax convoluted, when in fact it is a mode of expression perfectly suited to its environment—this dense jungle, this poverty, and this climate of extremes. That it has no natural way of saying "carburetor" or "nose job" does not dim its brilliance any more than the lack of a word that adequately describes the storm from which we had just escaped qualifies English's.

Sana meekly went to another darkened corner of the room and prepared dinner, joined by her worried husband. Still wet, I approached the feeble fire. The old woman turned away and the kids gathered around their sick brother.

It was nearly incomprehensible to me that a family could live in such squalor. What was shocking was not so much that the place was suffocatingly small—I knew three graduate students who paid $900 a month to share a studio that size on East 70th Street—but that it was in such extravagant disrepair. The plasterboard walls were near collapse and the floor was slimy with some sort of mold. The only ventilation was through a makeshift fireplace whose chimney was constructed from a flimsy metal sluice. The monsoon dripped in, never, it seemed, from the same leak twice.

The hut was furnished at random. The backseat of an automobile served as the hag's throne. An oil drum hung loosely over a water basin. The wall decorations consisted of a cheap tapestry and a three-color print of an octagonal animist symbol representing the "eight fields of life." Serving as a hearth rug was a piece of thermal insulation. The oldest daughter set dishes on a wooden table whose base had once been encircled by high-tension cables. Our boots were dripping on a lurid green piece of material that may have been a swatch of Astroturf.

"Here I am," Leslie suddenly announced, emerging from behind the screen.

We were startled. For a moment I did not recognize her and her Caucasian body in the peasant's drab costume. And then it was as if she were naked, every arc in her torso accentuated in the wraparound in a way no native woman's planar, boyish body ever could be. I could see her nipples erupting beneath the sackcloth. Intuitively, she had known how to fasten the garment, thereby heightening the parody.

My discomfort was extreme. In the eyes of these people, she was godless, parading her body about like some slut from Broadway or Pigale or our capital's own Rue des Chrétiens. I sternly glanced at the peasant, but his eyes were already cast to the floor.

Leslie, her gross (actually an 8B) feet bare except for scarlet nail polish that shone with more power than the kerosene lamp that illuminated the room, hunkered next to the sick child and tickled his belly. "Hello, hello there you," Leslie whispered.

The child, his eyes glassy, his breathing labored, offered no response.

Leslie looked at me and lifted a strand of her hair. Absently, she said, "This weather gives me the frizzies."

## II

I was born in a French hospital in the capital of my country, but at the age of two was taken to Paris, where my father was stationed on behalf of my nation's newly independent government. Throughout my childhood and adolescence my parents would shuttle between the

First World, the Second and the Third, depending on the nature of the mission my father was performing for his people. With my brothers, however, I spent most of these years in Europe, enrolled in Swiss and British schools, visiting here only about once every three summers, but never forgetting that this was my home. At the time of my twenty-seventh birthday, when I was completing graduate school in New York, I computed that I had lived five years, ten months, and fifteen days among my countrymen.

My father was a small, intense fellow who favored atheism, dark suits, and cosmopolitan manners. Nevertheless, he was an uncompromising patriot and ensured, directly or through tutors, that at least once every day I was reminded of who I was and of whom my education was meant to serve. My mother, a former dancer in the national theater, required us to speak my nation's language whenever we were in her presence. From the age of ten, I read every issue of my uncle's newspaper, regardless of the length of time required for it to be airfreighted to me.

Throughout my youth, the nation to which my life was consecrated existed not as a few thousand square kilometers of geography, but as a segment of the temporal continuum. It would truly exist for me only when I reached my parents' ages; it was a country of adulthood.

Sex, of course, was also a country of adulthood, and one I would even more frequently contemplate. Despite the occasional visit in my youth—usually in the company of a professional guide—I did not take up residence there until I met Leslie, then a student at Columbia

University's School of Foreign Relations. She was bright and good-natured and destined to be in possession of a great many foreign relations. She was also guiltlessly materialistic and, well, a bit zaftig. She disliked curry and believed man has known no better breakfast than an Egg McMuffin, yet she never complained about life here; she'd try anything. As a Protestant and a feminist, she was philosophically opposed to leisure, and she had an office in our family compound where she prepared regional political analyses for the Rand Corporation and a "household hints" column for my uncle's newspaper.

Her modest (by Western standards) public manners were belied by her private daring, and the first year that I knew her I was in a condition of lust-crazed shock. I had never known anyone like her, and even after we had begun living together in Manhattan I still hadn't figured her out.

The first weekend we spent at her parents' home was supposed to be a separate-rooms affair. Leslie, however, never even bothered to muss her bed. A keen student of Western mores, I had almost expected this, but such an unabashed disregard of parental regulations was nevertheless upsetting; indeed, it virtually unmanned me, nearly removing the entire point of her intrigue. The house, though fabulously assessed by the local authorities, was tiny, and I imagined her family could hear every squeal of the bed. Worse, one evening Leslie caught me in the downstairs bathroom, right down the hall from where her mother was preparing dinner, and demanded a quickie while perched on the edge of the marble sink. There was a mirror on the medicine cabinet door, and also one the entire length of the opposite wall and another on the inside of the tub. Looking over her shoulder, I could see my face in the medicine cabinet, and beyond it my ass, and then these reflections shrinking down to the size of a few hundred angstroms, and throughout all this I could hear her mother dicing onions.

I ended up pushing her into the basin and nearly cracking her head on the medicine cabinet, and my knees buckled and I almost fell onto the cool, just-scrubbed, polygonally tiled floor. Leslie, however, said, "That was fun."

"Fun?"

"Wasn't it?" She grinned sweetly like a little kid and pulled up her jeans.

"That's a pretty odd way of putting it."

"No it isn't."

"Fun? You don't have sex for fun."

"You don't?"

"When your mother's right down the hall?"

"She doesn't care. We're consenting adults."

"For crying out loud. If you can't wait to have sex until your mother's out of earshot, you're not doing it for fun."

"Why not?" she asked mildly. "She *is* out of earshot. And she said dinner wasn't going to be ready till 6:30, so I figured we had time—"

"Scrabble is fun. TV is fun. You don't have sex for the same reasons."

"You can. There's nothing on this early. Besides, all these mirrors are sort of kinky."

Leslie's family, much to my annoyance, never seemed to catch on to the fact that I was Asian. Her father, a terrifyingly secular Unitarian minister with hands the size of my head, insisted at first on calling me "Paul." The one man-to-man talk we had—on my professional expectations—was conducted as we tossed an American football between us in his backyard. Twice as I attempted to explain the role of model formats in macroeconomics, the ball sailed through my hands and ended up in the shrubbery. And then, with a forced casualness, he asked me if I was a Marxist. This was at the dawn of the last decade in which such things existed. I began a complicated explanation of my country's unique socio-economic situation, its history, its resources, and its difficult regional position, and kept at it until he lost interest.

Now, just a bit further into the decade, I was spending my first full year back home. Although I held an important position in the Ministry of Economic Development, I was still obliged to perform some military service. Indeed, as a member of the elite, I had a duty toward the army, the guardian of the nation's independence, that was lifelong. Even while in my office in the crumbling concrete skyscraper across the street from the national assembly, I was under the command of Major General Ti (a cousin by marriage). From the time I was eighteen I had spent three months of every year with my unit at the border, where our peasant soldiers stared with indifferent hostility across the frontier at our neighbor's peasant soldiers, who stared back.

As an officer I was allowed the company of my

family, and Leslie had stayed with me the last two weeks of my recent tour. It was her idea. As the only white woman in camp, she gave the troops something to talk about, I'm sure, but I didn't care, for what they said had no effect on my authority. More of a concern was what my fellow officers were thinking. My friends virtually cut me off. I was excused from our late-night drunks. I was quarantined from all sex-related jokes. Their wives, some of whom I had known since we were children, whose families had known mine for centuries, forgot the warmth they had once shown me and ended whatever casual flirtations we had cultivated. They had all known I had married a Westerner, of course, but it was not until she showed up in camp, making herself comfortable in the officer's mess, walking around in jean cutoffs and those impossible curls, asking innocent questions in mangled Mamaroneck High School French, that my decision set me apart. Not one of the women offered my wife the slimmest chance of a friendship.

Leslie never noticed this ostracism. She was too busy "having the experience" (her oft-used, jarring expression; sometimes it made me wonder if I was an object of love or, like much else in this country, merely a detail in the composition of an "interesting" life). She rode on elephants and in tanks and was more curious about the technology of our relatively sophisticated communications facility than were most spies. She asked keen questions about routine maneuvers. As an enthusiastic though unskilled volunteer, she worked in the infirmary, where seriously ill and injured men were too self-conscious to moan in her presence.

I enjoyed her company, but having her watch me play soldier, and her delight in the harmless minutiae of military organization, made me feel like there was something basically dishonest in my life. My military duty meant more to me than she could understand.

Two years earlier, I had seen action in a border clash and had received commendations for bravery and leadership:

We were in the bush a few hours before dawn, undeniably lost in this leafy, wet, chaotic terrain that cannot hold the ink of a surveyor's pen. There had been skirmishing earlier in the week. We were all tensed for a fight. My soldiers did not want to kill as much as they wanted to spend their ammunition; a few rounds of bullets at three piastres a shot would be the most expensive consumption their lives would ever allow. We could hear bats in the woods and something else, too. It was at this moment, before anything happened, that I was overcome by a feeling of . . . well, I'm not sure, but let's call it destiny. After a lifetime of urban existence, I felt most powerful and most in control of myself here in this dank wilderness. I had my life and the lives of my men in my hands, but I was at peace. I could already smell blood, and the jungle had never before seemed so much like home. There was a click and a flash, and before I could even give the orders—not that I had any specific orders to give—my troops were on their bellies firing into the night and whooping like the Native Americans portrayed in Hollywood movies.

I myself got off a few shots, each departing from my rifle with a gentle kick. One seemed to kick twice, as if it could transmit back to me the impact of its collision. My soldiers gleefully insisted that I had killed a man. When we returned to the area the next morning, we found several bodies. They had suffered a week's worth of decomposition in this rancid climate. I could hardly believe they had ever known life. It was only my respect for army regulations that made me turn down my sergeant's suggestion that I take home a foot as a trophy.

## III

We were served dinner, a thin rice porridge, on chipped plastic dishes emblazoned with the Esso tiger. The company, which had first offered them as premiums to encourage the American consumption of its gasoline, had been stuck with them after the 1973 oil boycott. A sharp Kuwaiti businessman bought them at a trivial price and earned a handsome profit in a deal with Joseph the Syrian, the richest man in the capital, who in turn sold the dishes to provincial distributors, mostly Indians, who made a killing in the local bazaars. Highly ranked in our pantheon of animal gods, the tiger is a creature of profound meaning to our countrymen, despite his near extinction in our heavily hunted jungles (his hides are paid for with hard currency).

Leslie and I sat on two straw mats while the peasant couple stood behind us a few meters away like the waiters at Tour d'Argent. Sana's face was hard as she stared beyond me at the still figure on the pallet. The children and their grandmother watched us from near the tiny fire. The family was quiet, stricken by anxiety, and not only because of the ill child.

My wife was undisturbed by this native scrutiny. When she visited the capital's outdoor food market near the docks, refusing the company of our servants, she was always followed by several small, startled boys at about fifteen paces. She would pretend not to notice them.

"Very good," Leslie complimented the peasants in their native tongue.

Krik stared. A stranger's benediction was usually a thrill for our peasants, but hearing our language spoken by this curly-haired enigma was completely numbing. My people were no more accustomed to hearing a white person speak our language than they were to conversing with a giraffe; perhaps they were even less accustomed.

Our meal ended with a series of tiny, painful coughs from behind us. Sana hurried to the pallet, where the child had spit up. Leslie quietly joined her. The spit, I noticed with vague encouragement, was clear. Sana lifted the child and wiped his face with a cloth pulled from a fold in her wrap. I pushed away my dish and one of the girls picked it up. She did not look at me.

"Now will you help my child?" Krik asked.

"I told you, I can't. I'm not a doctor."

"Please, your honor," he said, using a feudal term that had been outlawed for more than thirty years.

I turned away.

Leslie offered the woman a sympathetic but helpless smile. The woman stared back at her, waiting for something more. The child stirred unhappily in his mother's arms and opened his mouth as if he wanted to cry. My country's infant mortality rate, as measured by the

World Health Organization, was 130.4 deaths within one year per thousand live births.

"Milk?" Leslie suggested, desperate to tell Sana something, but not quite pronouncing the word correctly.

Herself desperate to understand, the mother continued to stare. Of course, I could have explained Leslie's meaning to her, but at the time did not think of it. I had already decided that there was nothing we could do and was reflecting on the idea that Americans always thought there *was* something they could do, if only by the virtue of their being Americans. This was one reason why they had built a great industrial society, yet also why at that moment the society was bedeviled by the consequences of what shouldn't have been done, the half-assed solutions for problems—such as foreign Communist insurgencies and empty deposit bottles of Coke—that it shouldn't have attempted to solve.

Leslie repeated what she had said, this time cupping her own breasts. Sana at last understood and picked up a nursing bottle from beside the pallet. Four kids at twenty-two—well, I could see why she used a bottle. And Leslie thought sex was fun.

The child, however, refused the milk. He would not suck. Sana repeatedly pushed the latex nipple into his mouth, but the thin, pale lips ignored it.

"Please," Sana begged the boy.

A little milk dripped from the bottle, but he immediately coughed it up. The woman shot my wife a glance of reproach.

"We've got to help him," Leslie said.

"Try a real breast."

"That's not the problem. He won't take anything."

"It probably was the problem. Or at least a problem. They can't get fresh milk here, or even any liquid formula in bulk, and the only running water is what's pouring down now out of the Vault of Menasha. I know this district. It's like twenty others in this province. They're working the hell out of a single stream or some goddam hole in the ground that was dug fifty years ago. You'll have the trots in the morning, I promise you."

"He's burning up. He might die."

"I see."

"What should we do?"

"I don't know. I'm sorry." I really was. Outside my office window there was a billboard the size of an ocean liner, the third side of the triangular plaza bordered by the government administration building and the national assembly. A mother rapturously gazed at the child in her arms, both oblivious to the traffic below them, an Asian pietà except that the child was alive and his fat little hands were about to seize a plastic bottle. The powdered formula was not only cheap at the dock, it was cheap to transport into the far provinces. I knew the figures well. The woman painted on the billboard was of some vague Eastern ethnicity, perhaps Thai, but her teeth and optimism were clearly imported from the West. It was the optimism that was really for sale.

Leslie asked Sana if there was medicine of any kind in the house. The woman sadly shook her head.

"He's dehydrated," Leslie murmured to me. "If we

can get some water in him, even to wet his lips . . . how about if we heat a bath and try to break the fever?"

"A bath?"

"We'll just keep wetting him to cool his body. My mother did it for me when I had the mumps."

"They wouldn't have nearly enough water, not in that drum."

"How much water would we need? Anyway, we can use rainwater."

The peasants witnessed this incomprehensible exchange with due solemnity. It was the closest they'd come to a medical consultation. They had an almost blind faith in Western and Western-trained doctors despite the fact, unknown to hardly anyone but a few historians, that my people were practicing an advanced and humane indigenous medicine when Europeans were still letting blood. We had no shamans; taking care of our own health was as natural as making our own breakfasts. Nowadays, with the infusion of Western medical practices and values, it was virtually against the law.

When I started to explain about the bath to Krik, however, his eyes narrowed. The old woman growled. The peasants would not trust me, even though I was dedicated to improving their lives. It was the accent, the urban posture, the styling I had gotten at the Hilton barbershop in the capital three months earlier . . . Meanwhile, Leslie was holding their ill son, and had now begun singing "Puff, the Magic Dragon." The other kids overcame their shyness, approached her, and were enormously pleased when she allowed them to touch her hair. My people had always been like that. Warily parochial in our judgment of each other, we had opened our arms to our conquerors: the Chinese, the French, the Japanese, the British, and now the UN, IMF, and Comecon bureaucrats.

"No," Krik stammered.

"What?

"Please, your honor. I have made a vow. My child's soul, no *baptême.*"

Well, now I just had to laugh. The one goddam word he knew in French.

"Don't be ridiculous."

"Your honor, I beg you."

"Just listen to me. I'm not a Christian."

"I promised my father I wouldn't allow it."

"Your boy is sick. He has too much heat inside him. The heat is part of the sickness. The water will draw it out."

"No."

"It's just a bath. You've taken baths before, haven't you?"

"I can't break my vow," he said sorrowfully. "Don't you understand?"

Sana suddenly stepped in front of him, her eyes glowing.

"Do it," she said. "I don't care. Just save my boy."

"You've got it all wrong," I protested.

"Don't talk to us like children. Just save him."

"This is going to help him, I swear."

"I told you that you can do it," she said evenly. "Go ahead then. Make him well."

For a moment, I thought of saying no. But that would have been of no use, it was a done deal. Under my direction, Krik and the older children placed some buckets, a tightly woven basket, and even an automobile hubcap at the doorway. In tremendous spiritual torment, Krik stared into the demon-ridden night. The storm blew in his face and past him into the shack. As the containers filled he passed them in, where the water was transferred to a pot, warmed over the fire, and then emptied into a basin by the grandmother's seat. Leslie occasionally tested the temperature of the water with her hand while Sana held the baby in her arms, slowly rocking him and gently singing a lullaby that I had never known. It took us a while to adequately fill the basin and get it properly lukewarm. Krik returned from the doorway not only soaked, but exhausted, as if the water clinging to his body were his own sweat.

Sana deferred to my wife, allowing her to place the naked child into the bath. The boy did not even blink as he was immersed. Leslie gently held him by the back, with one hand cradling his head. The entire family, save for the crone muttering to herself in another corner, intently watched the child and the white woman.

Leslie bobbed the boy in the water, splashing him and caressing his body with her wet hands. I paced, too nervous to stand around the basin. I wondered if Krik had any dry tobacco, but I did not ask. I was afraid of Sana. I was stirred as well. Her body was bent and wasted and her hair was the texture of straw, yet the blood fiercely rushing to her haggard face a moment ago had briefly recalled her recent youth. One could see what she had been like before she had four children. She leaned forward to watch Leslie and her thighs tensed against her housedress. Give her some teeth and a week at Club Med and she'd be okay. I could have married her.

The infant suddenly cried, startling us. It was a short bawl, but the clearest sound he had made all evening. "I think that's a good sign," Leslie said.

I hunkered to the basin and felt the child's forehead. As I did so, I thought perhaps he watched my hand. "But he's still hot."

"Well, it takes time."

"He's very hot."

"I know," Leslie admitted. "But let's keep on doing it. If we can get his fever down a degree or two and get him to drink something, I think he'll make it until the doctor arrives."

I was silent for a moment as she ladled more water onto the boy's flat, tawny chest.

"Doctor? There's not going to be any doctor."

"But you said—"

"There's not going to be any doctor," I repeated furiously.

Her face stiffened. "You said they sent for one."

"Sure, but they won't get him. Not in this weather. They probably wouldn't get him anyway. I thought that was obvious. You think the army has so many doctors to spare? Or so many jeeps?"

"But hell," she said. "How far is Sempril anyway?"

"It's just down the mountain."

"That doesn't make any sense."

Still holding the child, she turned to Krik and asked, "Why is it that your father-in-law went to Pat'in?"

"The postmaster has a radio there," Krik explained earnestly. "He can call to Sempril for a doctor."

"But don't you understand, citizen?" I interrupted, reasserting my military, political, and social authority by the introduction of this salutation. "The army cannot dispatch a doctor every time someone's child falls ill. And nothing can move out in that storm. You don't even know if the old man made it to Pat'in."

"My son," he began helplessly as the rest of the family looked on.

Damn these peasants.

"Sempril's only thirty kilometers away. And the road isn't quite that bad. You could have bundled up the child and sent him there. If the old man had left with him yesterday morning, they could have made it to the camp by midday and missed the brunt of the storm."

"My son," the peasant began again.

"Your son," I said sarcastically. "Why didn't you send your son to Sempril?"

Very quietly Krik said, "There is no grace on the road."

Meaning: if a person dies while traveling, his spirit must first journey through the bush and find its way home before ascending to what is, roughly, my people's idea of heaven. For the soul of an infant, such a difficult passage might well prove impossible. I blew up.

"You jackass," I said in English before finding the proper epithets of my own language.

"You're an idiot! How can medicine help you if you continue to think like a savage? How can science, how can technology, how can *anything* help you?"

"Honey, we're guests—"

"It's your fault if your child dies," I told Krik. "You could have saved him."

My anger made me dizzy. I stalked away from the basin. The nails of my clenched fists dug into my palms.

After a while, Leslie resumed bathing the infant while Sana watched anxiously, glancing up from time to time at me and her husband, who had been humiliated in his own home. The entire family had been shocked by my outburst, even the old woman. The eldest girl had tears in her eyes. I leaned against a damp plasterboard wall and stared at the cold concrete floor. I refused to pity these people, my country, or myself.

## IV

Did the hours tick away? No, there was no clock. The rain falling—that is, crashing, drumming, rattling, popping, hissing, and, if you will, ringing like a spill of coins—on the tin-paneled section of the roof marked the only passage of time. It was a time that could not be represented by the even sweep of a second hand, nor that of an hour hand, nor by the publication of calendars nor by the magnetic resonance of cesium. It came in floods. In a roar. First a second, then a century. History was only a sequence of events and if nothing happened—as nothing here ever did—no time has passed at all. Krik and Sana could have been as old as the temple at Mukrent, but mere infants compared to the Citicorp Building.

Two of the small children slept together on a piece of foam insulation, the head of one against the shoulder of the other. A third child watched them. Krik sat against a wall, his arms around his twisted knees. Sana and Leslie took turns bathing the child and did not attempt conversation. Sana's mother stared into the fire while sitting in the backseat of an automobile whose front could have been thousands of miles away. I found a rag and cleaned my pistol.

The child's cry had no reprise. Leslie stared past him. After an indefinite period in which the rest of us were soothed by the untextured noise of the storm, she said, mostly to herself, "I wish I were a doctor. My parents wanted me to go to medical school."

"Medical school?" I asked mildly. "Do you think many children of my nation have been saved by American medical schools?"

She shrugged. "A few. Anyway, I would save this one."

"Maybe," I allowed. "But this child doesn't need a doctor—a whole doctor, that is—any more than he needs piano lessons. He may even need piano lessons more. Sure, a medical doctor trained in the West, after about a hundred grand in personal tuition fees and government subsidies, has many skills, including one or two that would help this kid, but ninety-nine percent of the stuff is irrelevant. Most of it is irrelevant to anything but making money. Mumbo jumbo so that every MD in a BMW sounds like a scientist. They come here with their CAT scanners, their centrifuges, their pills they get as samples from the pharmaceutical multinationals, and their self-righteous do-gooding, and they turn health into a commodity. My people can't afford to think of health as something to be purchased, or even as a tangible gift. What this kid needs is fresh milk, decent food, and a few shots. Two of these items were in abundance in my country long before anyone in your medical schools had ever heard of us, back before we were told progress had to be imported. The average life span of my people has actually dropped in the last sixty years. But what's the point of living longer anyway? What's the point of saving this kid if this is the brute existence in store for him?"

"Well," Leslie said. "I still wish I could break this fever."

"I wish I could teach the kid to play the piano."

Leslie turned away and sprinkled some bathwater into the child's face. "C'mon, fella," she mumbled.

The boy blinked. I wasn't quite sure I had seen it until he did it again. The flicker of a smile lit Sana's face for a moment. My wife managed to find the words to ask her to reheat some water. The woman, who perhaps thought the above harangue was the baptismal invocation, did as she was told without hesitation.

"You see, I think it's working."

"It's not going to be enough," I said. "The fever's only a symptom. The kid has an infection. He really needs something like penicillin. And it's probably even too late for that."

"Dammit, we haven't been thinking. Isn't there a case of first aid stuff in the jeep?"

"There's gauze in it and some antivenom, and that's all," I responded sullenly. I had, in fact, made an attempt to properly stock it the day before, as we were preparing for our return, but the infirmary was low on supplies. The chief physician had not been content merely to give this message to an orderly, but had made the walk over to our quarters to tell it to me himself. He was apologetic but earnest in his plea that I use my influence in the capital to get his requisitions fulfilled. He had probably oversold to the black market and been caught short.

"In your shaving kit," Leslie said and snapped her fingers, a gesture that usually amused me. "There's some Bufferin in your shaving kit. I'm almost sure of it."

"It won't help him," I said, shaking my head. "This boy needs a lot more than a Bufferin."

Krik pulled himself up from the floor and hobbled out of the room's shadows. His jaws were locked shut. He clenched his fists.

"Buff'rin," he said, revealing that the son of a bitch knew yet another foreign word. "You have Buff'rin?"

"It's in the jeep and it won't help your son anyway. Sending him to Sempril might have helped, but the Bufferin is useless."

"It might bring the fever down," Leslie said in English.

"Get it," the peasant demanded.

"It wouldn't hurt to go back for it."

"In that storm? No way."

"Your honor, you must," the man said. For a moment I thought he was going to lunge at me. I rested a hand on my holster.

"I beg you," Sana said to Leslie, who nodded in sympathy, affirming a naive belief in the solidarity of gender, rather than class or nation.

Then Leslie declared, "I'll get it."

"No you won't. You'd never make it. You were out there, you know what it's like, and now it's night and the storm's even worse. You'd never find your way there and back. None of us would."

It was a stalemate, and we were all silent for a moment. Then Sana went to the back of the room and withdrew something from one of the cartons. I knew what it was. She did not look at me as she returned, her hands clutched to her chest, her steps measured, to the time kept by some inaudible nuptial march: my bride.

I backed away, horrified. The child's soul, taken by baptism, was not enough?

In her hands were two soiled notes, ten dollars apiece.

"Here, she said. "It's all we have."

I raised my hands, opened them flat, and shook them at her, and further retreated so that my back was against the wall. Still she advanced, trembling, intent on touching me with the filthy money. My mouth was open but I could not at first speak, as if with all my polyglot skills I had forgotten the rudiments of manufacturing human speech. Then, in English, I yelled, "No, you don't understand!"

"Save my child," she begged, waving the hard currency about as if she wanted to beat me with it.

"No," I cried again, but I grabbed my army raincoat, threw it on my shoulders, shoved my feet into my boots, and, without even lacing them or saying anything more, I flung open the door and ran out into the storm.

# V

This is what happens: the tropical summer sun heats the land and the ocean unequally, the sea absorbing a far greater quantity of solar radiation. The land gives up the heat it cannot absorb to the atmosphere above it, which then expands and rises, creating a draft of dense ocean air. This parcel of air carries the ocean's evaporated moisture and the latent heat absorbed from the sun. As it moves inland, the ocean air rises and the water vapor condenses into raindrops. The precipitation releases the latent heat, further buoying the column and further intensifying the draft. A monsoon is thus a huge machine that transforms solar energy into potential energy and then, with dramatic effect, converts the potential energy into the kinetic energy of wind and rain. For this explanation I am indebted to Peter J. Webster, writing in the August 1981 issue of *Scientific American* (which is dedicated to forging an entire nation of them!).

Or, conversely: one summer, when the earth and man were young and not yet in their current forms, when the number of things that were possible was greater than the number of things that were not, Pen the hunter left his beautiful wife, Tal, in order to hunt the jungle for the most succulent deer and young boar. His quiver stocked with a thousand arrows so sharp he could not see their points, he marched deep into the jungle, unafraid and arrogant, deeper than any man should go. But soon he was ignoring the fine game virtually underfoot, for he had heard the song of the Wild Princess, promising him everything he had ever wanted or had thought he wanted. He followed it to the near bank of the one river and found her there, combing her tresses, and he was enchanted. She took him to her bed, which was made entirely of the light reflected off the river on the day of the summer solstice, while Menasha, the tiger-king, watched from his celestial lair. Pen's ecstatic moans, transported into the winds by the wings of a thousand sparrows, reached the ears of Tal, who burst from her home weeping and begged the jungle to return her faithless husband. As she stood unprotected in the clearing in front of her house, Menasha appeared, took the woman between her jaws, and in one leap carried her to his empire of the heavens, where he placed her as a treasured prize in his vault, whose walls are a thousand bricks high and a thousand bricks deep. Despite Menasha's charm and, quite frankly, his virility, Tal still wishes to be with her husband and each summer cries for him, and on behalf of the suffering of all the world's women. Her tears flow so heavily they seep through the masonry, and her wails stir both the sky and the earth. For the above account I make grateful acknowledgement to Lester R. Fernald, author of *Myths and Legends of the Eastern Peoples,* Vol. II (London: Hurst and Blackett, 1937).

Less than thirty running paces from the peasants' hovel, I had tripped over my sodden army coat. As I staggered to my feet, the entire sky heavy on my back, my clothes remained rooted to the earth. I stood there for a while, my body rocked one way and then another in the torrent, and I wondered if I would really make it to the jeep or if I would hear Leslie if she called into the night for me to return. Without thinking, I shrugged off the coat, allowing it to be claimed by the bubbling soil, which was as pungent as blood.

The loss of weight was invigorating. I peeled off my boots and my muddy socks. I unbuckled my holster and casually dropped it, an act for which I could have been court-martialed. Undressing as quickly as any lover, I shucked off my uniform trousers, my shirt, and my Jockey briefs, and with each garment thrown into the mud, I felt myself stronger, and even buoyant. I held the keys to the jeep in my right hand. I was completely naked, but unilluminated, so that I could not see my body. For a moment, before I again engaged the storm, I felt as if I had no body at all.

I slogged my way down the road. My body was cut by wind-whipped bushes and branches, but the storm numbed the pain, and the blood ran freely and un-obtrusively into the graves of my ancestors. I repeated to myself, in three languages, the injunction to keep moving. I could not see, but my feet communicated with the edge of the road, and I trusted my heading.

The jungle was as dark as the bottom of the ocean, but no darker. Indefinite forms swam around me: man-eating animals, zombies, and the spirits of the dead or even worse; or common things, I told myself, like what scared you in a strange bedroom in the middle of the night.

Down the road, the jeep was only another of the jungle's black ghosts. From the moment I first thought I saw it, a while passed before I actually reached it, as if it were slowly rolling away or as if the deluge were diluting the space between us. The mud here was thick and each time I pulled a foot out of it there was a noise like a vaginal gasp on the upstroke. I almost fell when I reached the vehicle, but then I steadied myself and clinked the keys against it—metal against metal, the sound of civilization—discovering that it was indeed real.

Inside the jeep I opened my suitcase, which was part of the Samsonite luggage set that was our wedding gift from Leslie's grandparents. Like a thief, I frantically dug through my things: a dress uniform, polo shirts, a pair of jeans, tennis sneakers, and a two-week-old copy of the Asian *Wall Street Journal*. At the bottom of my suitcase I found my shaving kit, and inside it, next to the aerosol can of mentholated shaving cream, I found the Bufferin. The lather is the greater miracle: it heats itself after being dispensed from the can.

I tried to start the engine. It made no sound that could be heard above the storm. None of its dashboard indicators stirred. If it turned over I would have made it to the capital by dawn. The engine, however, was quite dead.

My feet slipped as I left the jeep. The tiny plastic container flew from my hands into the mud.

I found it, but only after several panicked minutes on my hands and knees, sifting the soil. The bottle was caked with dirt, yet its contents were clean. I could see through the mud the ball of brilliant white cotton that—in defiance of the instructions printed on the side of the container in six languages, none of them mine—I had left in the bottle as a token of the pills' purity and potency.

My return was directly against the direction of the storm. It no longer struck me as wind and rain, but as a single brutal force. I attempted to walk sideways to cut my exposure, but each time I opened my body to the storm, it found its advantage and whipped me around savagely. Only a hundred meters or so from the peasants' home, I slipped, fell hard, and slammed my head against a rock. My ankle turned. For about three seconds, the earth was dry and lit. "Mama," I cried.

I lay in the mud, trying to spin myself away from the pain. Perhaps it was not as bad as I now recall; after all, it was only a bump on the head and a twisted ankle. Nevertheless, I had been defeated, and defeated not only in the efforts of that night. Naked and helpless in the land of my birth, I had made no progress at all. I was a prisoner of the jungle, and whatever spirits held dominion over it.

*"Notre Père qui es aux Cieux,"* I began, praying to the power of the Jesuits who had run the school I had attended outside Geneva. I remembered crisp linen and a lay teacher's aftershave. But I knew that if there was a God in heaven, even he would be unable to see through the storm, so I also prayed to Menasha, who might be right there in the bushes, behind a tree, swaying from a branch above me or perhaps in a low-lying fold in the clouds.

Menasha is neither good nor bad; he is, however, capricious and powerful. It pays to court him and, if necessary, to exhort, provoke, intimidate, charm, bribe, and beg him. Wear him down and soften him up. Appeal to his good side. Appeal to his bad side. Flatter, demand, play on his sympathies. Don't hope for what you want, and then maybe you'll get it, but not if this thought has already occurred to you. Unexpect the expected.

After a while I tried to stand, but under the force of the storm, it was much easier to walk in a crouch or even crawl. And so I crawled, the Bufferin in my left hand, the keys to the jeep cutting into the palm of my right. I kept my head down and slowly made my way.

According to native belief (Fernald, *ibid.*), man had once walked on all fours and had lived a happy life that way in harmony with the other inhabitants of the jungle. On his knees, he could see the world much clearer than he does now. He was glad to feed on the grapes that fell from the vines in the Wild Princess's arbor. The grapes still on the vines were for the princess only, but the jungle animals were welcome to whatever lay on the ground. So much fell that no animal was ever hungry, or even knew what hunger was, but man grew bored with this easy life and was irritated that he should be treated in the same way as the other animals. He wanted the grapes on the vine—if only because the other animals could not have them. When no one was looking, he nibbled at the vines near the ground and, after getting away with that, he reached for the grapes a little above his head. In truth, these grapes tasted no better than the ones that had fallen, and some were sour because they had not been allowed to ripen, but man was thrilled to do what was forbidden. He mistakenly believed that the grapes directly off the vine had given him special powers of perception and immunity to retribution. These beliefs made him reckless, and one day, in full view of the world, he reached the top of the arbor and attempted to pull down a thousand bunches of a thousand grapes each, more than he could possibly eat. As he stretched, the Wild Princess furiously struck him with a sapling, paralyzing his body in that position, so from that day on he would be forced to stand on two feet, never sure of his balance. Then with the sapling she tickled his unprotected stomach, so from that day on he would always be hungry.

As I crawled, I could see how unsuited an upright posture was to this climate. On all fours, my body was secure and somewhat sheltered from the storm's power. Bipedalism was just another example of inappropriate technology transfer.

Crawling, however, would not ensure my acceptance by the jungle. The storm still beat on my back and head, and into my eyes whenever I tried to look up. I thought of Menasha and the other creatures of the bush. It was unlikely, I knew, for any of them to be about in this fierce weather, but I could not help but think of the leopard we had killed while we were on patrol a few weeks earlier. My sergeant shot it before it sensed our approach. Then, with one bullet from my revolver, I killed the antelope the leopard had been eating. The leopard preferred its prey alive, the heart still pumping blood. It had been eating the antelope from the rear, chewing into its bowels and up into its body. As I approached it, the antelope's pain-moistened eyes watched me carefully. Shocked into sentience, it was fully conscious of its fate, and of what constituted mercy. The image of these two creatures, one's body halfway up the other's—the leopard trying to slip into an antelope suit—haunted me as I crawled along the side of the road, my own ass bare and vulnerable.

And I was alone against the other demons: wild dogs, poisonous spiders, and mosquitoes that can swell to the size of your thumb while sucking your blood. Certain species of vulture will tear the eyes out of a living man. The Penta snake crawls into a man's ear and forces him to hear every evil thought in the world. The single bite of Har the lizard puts a man to sleep for a thousand days. When he awakes, his body is entirely infested with worms. After midnight in the rainy season, Har's victims can be seen wandering through the countryside.

And then, of course, there was the Wild Princess . . .

It was by the application of all my will that I continued my progress into the storm, and also by the invocation of certain memories. I recalled the expression of a very young girl ice-skating at Rockefeller Center a few Decembers before. I had stood alone at the railing above the rink, across from the bronze figure of Prometheus, warm in my trench coat, almost intoxicated by the dry air of a newly arrived cold front. I had never seen the girl before and she would never see me, for she danced oblivious to all but the ice and her balance. She skated backwards, she leaped, she spun, yet I hardly noticed her glittering movements, so intent was my study of her face. It showed, in its vivid, rapturous self-control, that the girl had conquered the physical. This human triumph encouraged me more than all the world's machines. All our science, our literature, and our art—everything we had done with the gift of fire—was not as impressive as the set of her jaw and the transparency of her eyes. Despite the pre-Christmas tumult around me, I was at ease. I was safe in the heart of the world.

But then I could not remember the girl any more than I could remember what I had dreamed before I was born. Rockefeller Center had been destroyed in the monsoon.

## VI

As I reached the hovel, I found my muddy coat and covered myself with it. Inside, the austere tableau was little changed from before. Leslie, the small children, and Sana's mother were by the fire, Krik brooded on his haunches in another corner, and Sana, with the oldest girl in attendance, held the baby in her arms, rocking him above the pallet. The single significant difference in the setting was that the room was partitioned by a long cotton sheet. A three-stroke ideogram, whose translation would require a commentary of such length that, attending it, the reader could easily forget the scene I'm attempting to describe, was painted on charcoal on each side of the sheet.

Once inside the door and free of the storm's weight, I feebly raised the Bufferin for display.

My wife's look was sorrowful.

"I know," I said before she could speak. "The sheet."

My ankle sore, I limped to the fire and grabbed a rag to dry myself. The children and their grandmother scattered as I approached, and I was overcome by a powerful tremor. Although I stood on the short hearth, I felt no heat. I sat down heavily. Leslie did not touch me.

Sana stared into the face of the infant, seeing something visible to herself alone.

"Where's your clothes?" my wife asked at last, confining her query to a solemn whisper.

"They weighed me down. That's how it is with us."

We watched the fire. The old woman placed three greasy candles on the child's pallet.

"It's not really your fault," Leslie said after a while.

"'Really'?" I cried. "It's not 'really' my fault? It's not by any stretch of the imagination my fault. He should have sent the kid to Sempril."

"I just mean you were away so long—"

"I made it in record time. You don't know what it's like out there."

From the carton that had produced the identity papers and the hard currency, Krik now removed a Bic lighter. He handled it carefully. Not quite adept at the proper flicking motion, he stroked it several times before managing to ignite it. As the old woman moaned the traditional incantations, Krik squatted by the candles and lit them.

"All right," Leslie said. "Just calm down."

Calm down. It wasn't my fault. Krik should have sent the kid to Sempril. Sana should not have used untreated water to mix the formula. The district authority should regulate the use of its rivers and wells. The central government should better organize the region's resources. Condensed formula should not be sold in areas that are without appropriate water supplies. Our people should practice birth control. The government, my government, should assure them that it, and not their

litters of children, will support them in their old age—
even though it can't.

Our people must be educated to live like men, something they once knew as well as any other nation. My
country cannot overcome the jungle. It is the jungle. But
it must find a place for itself somewhere in this world
and in this century of ruthless miracles.

"I've had enough," I told Leslie, and I grabbed her
by the arm so that she could help me up. I had already
picked a spot to sleep, a dry corner on the other side of
the sheet. "Let's go to bed."

She pulled away.

"The mourning. They explained it to me."

"The hell with it," I said, standing on my own.

Native tradition and belief demanded, among other
things, the separation of the sexes the night after a death
in the home. Hence the sheet. Man and woman were
not to touch each other, not even to provide comfort.
This was to prevent a defilement of the dead's spirit, and
also to prevent any undestined conception that might
trap the departing soul in another miserable earthbound
existence.

"Come on," I said.

Leslie stood but shook her head, studying my bare
feet. She still wore Sana's coarse wraparound. "No."

"Jesus," I said, my voice raised before the grieving,
uncomprehending family. "Did they explain the rest to
you? The keening and the bowing and the tearing of the
already well-torn clothes? How about the salt gargle and
the body paint? Did they explain how the heat from the
candles buoys the spirit to its final destination, which is

not quite heaven, but a jungle without fear or chaos? Do you believe this crap?"

"I don't believe it—"

"But you respect it. You find it interesting. No, you find it colorful. My country's colorful peasants. This death is for your benefit, to entertain you, to inform you about my people's primitive religious beliefs and ceremonies."

"How can you say that? How about the family's feelings? Where's your compassion?"

"With the kid," I said, catching hold of one of her wrists. "I don't respect the way he died, nor do I find it colorful."

My weight fell on the twisted ankle but I held on to her, the pain only intensifying my grip.

"You're hurting me," she said, absolutely confused. I had never before used force against her; if I had done this in New York, she would have left me without giving it a second thought. Now she did not know how to respond nor how frightened to be, alone in this cruel land. I gripped her harder, slowly turning her whitened arm, mindlessly looking for the first sign of tears in her eyes, around which, I just then noticed, there were still somehow traces of black mascara.

I was tired but I did not sleep. Nor did Leslie, who lay next to me on a vinyl mat, covered by a thin army blanket. She made neither a sound nor a sign, but I imagined I knew every thought in her head.

The unsteady candles cast grotesque shadows onto the sheet, which was tied to an in improvised second sheet at the middle to divide the peasants' half of the room. We were alone, on the other side. Limbs stretched the length of the sheet and then bubbled off from their torsos. Separate writhing figures suddenly became one. Penumbras joined and gave birth to tiny, unrecognizable shadows. The projections were clearly not those of the body; they belonged to the extreme postures of the spirit. Nor did the cries of my countrymen seem human. They were without design. Although the mourning songs were in my language, and I had been taught them as part of my cultural upbringing, I could not understand the words. Indeed, there were no words, just bits of noise that meant nothing alone, but when taken together meant more than words could express. It was magic. It was *my* spirit that was being mourned, that would be lifted to the wet skies by the heat of the peasants' sorrow.

It must have been near dawn when they finally stopped, bedding down in their segregated quarters. The rain continued to assault the hovel, and the wind moaned, also mourning. Eclipsed, my country would never see the day. I reached to my wife, my hands gently finding her smooth, round belly. She flinched just once under my touch. I made love to her without pleasure, violently and audibly, as if I were not making love to her at all, but were burrowing inside her, searching for a place to live.

# A Line Is a Series of Points

The morning opens with a song that has never been heard before. It rises from the sands like heat and descends upon the head of the column. As the song ripples back along the spine of the march, it is transformed, with added lyrics and a more complicated melody.

This is the song just before it reaches us:

"The road lies beneath
And soars above.
Humma-hummmm.
We walk the road only in part."

Then the song washes over our section of the column, and we add to it:

"The road is a line.
A line is a series of points."

Our voices rise, mix, and negotiate a harmony, reminding us that we are a people. And then the song leaves us. We close our parched lips. The song is picked up behind us, slightly altered, so that it has an extra beat in every other line, plus a refrain. The refrain is:

"Shumma shumma shummmm . . ."

And then the song is gone forever, just as our footprints disappear into the sand every night.

No one can say precisely how long we have been walking or what fraction of the earth's surface we have traversed. We have walked long enough for many of us to have married and borne children; also, enough time for others, embittered by the rigors of the march, to have divorced, even though they continue to walk on parallel tracks. Our old and sick die every night and are left behind every morning in unmarked, unrecorded graves. Once we turn our backs the ground behind us appears undisturbed. Aid workers often ask us who our leaders are, or who sets our direction, or who decides when we should bed down for the night, or who decides when we should get going once more in the morning, or, at the very least, who can sign receipts for relief supplies. We can't reply to these questions with any certainty, or even say that we know where we're going.

When we left our homes we told ourselves that we would return in a few hours, once the fighting died down, or by the following day, or by the end of the week. We extinguished the lights in our front rooms without taking with us the memories of these rooms, we shut our doors without looking back, and we walked through our front gates without recalling the childhoods lived in our gardens and yards. Now we can no longer recall what our homes looked like, or whether they were of clapboard or brick or built on one floor or two, or what time of day the postman made his deliveries.

We walk under a high thin sky that fades imperceptibly into the bleached terrain, so that we rarely see the horizon, and the flatness of the land hides the column's head, its tail, and tomorrow's place of encampment. Some of us, especially the young men, run ahead to the front of the column, but they never return to report what they have found there. Others, such as the old, lag behind, and they too never return. Those who were ahead of us and then fell behind until they reached our section of the column speak of the head of the column with some authority, but their gossip is always stale, like the data borne by the spectra of stars hundreds of light-years away. They can't tell us anything about the territory we're about to enter because they haven't been there. They aren't actually moving back to us: we're catching up with them.

News instead comes from our songs, which always roll back along the column from its head:

> "The shadow of a creek,
> The thorn tree's fear,
> A sand grain's memory.
> We turn left at the grassy hillock,
> The trees are stripped bare."

Jetliners rumble above the desert, making the twice-weekly Manila-Bombay-Almaty-Dakar-Montevideo run. Many of us pause for a moment, if only to enjoy the spectacle of something in the sky besides the sun and the stars. Children wave. Perhaps the passengers look from their windows and observe the black river snaking through the dead lands, and they may idly ask themselves the name of the country they are flying above.

Sometimes a jet will leave a vapor trail that beckons like a road sign.

Late every afternoon a line of disturbed air in the distance runs parallel to the column's march. Dust devils dance against the haze. What first appears to be a black claw scraping at the edge of the earth resolves into a small fleet of all-terrain vehicles. Before night has completely obscured the desert, a settlement of tents and vans has sprouted around us, populated by relief workers. They are handsome men and women with large, white teeth. Unfortunately, they're often in much worse health than we are, afflicted by mosquito bites, sunburn, frostbite, diarrhea, and dehydration. We offer them our traditional remedies. When we wake at morning twilight they're gone, only to reappear at our next stop. Or perhaps they're not the same relief workers: we never recognize individual doctors or nurses.

Within the column itself we are without advanced medicine, not even aspirin, nor gauze for bandages, nor syringes; whatever the relief workers leave is stolen or misplaced. Beyond our sight, traveling parallel to our column and the aid mission, is a kind of mobile village founded by merchants who sell the stolen relief supplies to the indigenous population and the local authorities. Hospitals and clinics in the countries through which we pass momentarily prosper, and life expectancy figures surge. They subside after we move on.

It's said that the financial capital generated by the sale of these relief supplies has established *another* traveling village several kilometers further beyond the horizon. This village caters to the personal needs of the relief workers and the merchants in the first village, with restaurants, an appliance store, and a drugstore. This is only a rumor: all we know of the countries through which we pass is the sand directly beneath our feet. Other rumors suggest additional, more elaborate commercial centers tracing even more distant paths through the desert.

Some of us have bedrolls and mess kits, others nothing more than the shirts, trousers, and running shoes that we were wearing when we left home. Some walk barefoot, the skin of our feet as tough and brittle as bark. At night we repair our clothes, using for material empty sacks stamped *Red Cross* and *UNHCR.* By campfires up and down the column we hear prophecies of our destination: its green fields, its trout-filled streams, its gleaming cities. The place does not have a name, or if it does our seers are afraid to pronounce it. Naming the place would limit it to a point on a map that not a single one of us possesses. It would make the place merely a finite number of square kilometers, with a finite history and a finite future. To name our destination would turn our shamans into politicians.

The ground is hard and the nights are cold, yet our sleep is always restful. Once the relief workers have left and the campfires have burned down, the column is quiet. A few infants cry out, but they are quickly comforted. An elder snores; another's bones dully clatter as he stumbles down death's staircase. We reach out to each other to make love. The stars whirl above us.

On another day a rumor, or a story, or a tale, or a song, passes along the column:

"Humma-humma-humma.
The breeze that isn't the wind.
The echo beneath the sands.
The sky that darkens the day.
The flames that sear the night.
Hummmm.
An angle is the figure generated
By the intersection of two lines.
Listen."

The rumor is this: another column of refugees, from
another country and of another race, is also traveling
through the desert, in a direction that may bring it into
collision with our column. Some of us predict war and
we take from our packs any implements that could be
employed as weapons: spoons, sewing needles, sharp-
ened keys to abandoned automobiles. Our would-be
defenders are derided: what do we possess to fight over?
Nevertheless, the possibility of another people like us
has disturbed even the pacifists: the one thing we
thought we possessed was our *uniqueness*. We believed
that we held claim to the sum of the world's sympathy;
that we were paragons of misery; that ages hence poets
would employ our travails as a metaphor for all kinds
of alienation and displacement. It is unbearable to consider now that there may be another people, in equal or
even greater distress, with whom we must share our
symbolism.

This rumor is soon countered by another: Indeed, we
are the only refugees remaining in the world. Everyone
else has reached their homes. The world refugee problem

has been completely solved by the same kind of practical science and political determination that eradicated the smallpox virus. We are merely the exception or, like the smallpox germs that are kept frozen in a laboratory vault, we are the remnants of an epidemic being preserved for future study. The world will keep us homeless, if only to remind itself that there were once refugees.

And then there's yet another rumor: no, there *are* other columns of refugees, thousands of columns, everyone is a refugee. We are all lost, no one has a home—certainly not the exhausted relief workers nor their superiors in Geneva and New York, who fretfully track our passage on satellite photographs. The passengers riding the vapor trails above us will change planes disoriented and hungry, unsure whether the gray dusk outside the terminal belongs to the morning or evening star.

For weeks we sing of the approach of the other refugees. The songs become more precise in their definition of the others, as if we are molding them from our own music. We dream of the others: sometimes they are as beautiful as children, clad in robes of silk. Other times we wake in fear, chilled by the night. In the day our pace quickens, even though we're unsure whether we're hurrying toward comradeship or battle. And then one morning the other column appears perpendicular to our line of march, coming directly at us. Head on, it's impossible to gauge its size or distance. We stop and face them, our legs as heavy as stone, and the morning stretches into evening dusk as the two columns tremble before each other.

And then they arrive in a frenzied rush and we

realize, as we raise our hands in wary greeting, that this is the head of our own column, which has somehow circled back to cross the column's center. There is chaos for a quarter of an hour and then the renewal of old friendships, reconciliation, and great song making that lasts well into the night. By dawn the column has re-organized itself and resumed its course.

We hardly recall the place from which we came; all our songs refer instead to the place to which we are going. It is for this reason, and because we had been looking the other way when we departed, that none of us recognize the approach to our own country. Now we cross the river that we once called Mother and file into the valley named Heart and pass along the outskirts of the capital city that was once the vessel of our young people's ambitions. We know we're here. No one says, *this is home,* but our songs are replaced by a steady, wordless susurrus.

As we pass through villages and fields, the country's inhabitants halt their work. They don't speak, but merely stand by the side of the road, leaning against their farming equipment. Their faces are hard and their pitchforks look deadly. We file along, careful not to jostle each other out of the column. Some of us believe we recognize our former homes, but the recognition is as faint as the illusion of déjà vu. People come to the windows and stand in doorways, and we think we see our nephews and sisters-in-law, but we're not entirely sure. They offer us nothing in their slate gray eyes. It is as if they don't see the column at all.

And now we're not sure we have really recognized

either them or this country. These street names are unfamiliar; this country's climate is drier than we thought the climate had been at home; its music relies more heavily on electrically amplified string instruments; its macaroni dishes are undercooked; its children's tales revolve around a small, cunning pig, rather than the small, cunning rabbit with whom our children slide into sleep; we don't understand these people's jokes or their football strategies; they make love in postures we would find either uncomfortable or repellent; the billboards on the side of the highways are not in our own language, which has in the years of exile taken on the rhythms of the march and the grammar of the desert. In any event, tomorrow we will be somewhere else.

**KEN KALFUS** is an American writer who has lived in Paris, Dublin, and Belgrade. Since 1994, he has made his home in Moscow with his wife, Inga, and their daughter, Sky. This is his first collection of fiction.

You can contact Ken Kalfus at 72754.2514@compuserve.com and Kenkalfus@yahoo.com.

# Thirst

# Ken Kalfus

## ABOUT THIS GUIDE

The suggested questions are intended to help your
reading group find new and interesting angles
and topics for discussion for Ken Kalfus's *Thirst.*
We hope that these ideas will enrich your
discussion and increase your enjoyment of the book.

Many fine books from Washington Square Press
include Reading Group Guides. For a complete listing,
or to read the Guides on-line, visit
http://www.simonsays.com/reading/guides

## DISCUSSION QUESTIONS

1. In the two stories that make up "Le Jardin de la Sexualité," Ken Kalfus imagines Paris—through the eyes of a virginal, culturally prejudiced Irish au pair—as a city buzzing with a powerful undercurrent of lust and frank sexuality. Throughout "Bouquet" and "Thirst," chart the progress of Nula's relationship with Henri, the young Moroccan student. What images and metaphors does the author use to illustrate his vision of Paris?

2. In what ways do the characters and events in "Bouquet" and "Thirst" underscore and inform the following pairs of words: innocence and experience; West and East; science and sex; sublimation and desire; thirst and satisfaction.

3. "The Joy and Melancholy Baseball Trivia Quiz" delivers a fantastical, alternate history of our national pastime that's as dark and tragic as it is playful, comic, and absurd. What do each of these detailed recollections have in common with each other? Consider the narrator's simultaneously poignant and detached play-by-play regarding the foul-hitting champion's at-bat: "Each memory is telescoped inside another, as all would be at the end of life and, if the world of living things is lucky, as our lives would be left to us in death: remembering remembering remembering, and so on."

4. Describe the tone of "Cats in Space." What is the attitude of the narrator, whose adult job "sometimes requires brutality, in a quiet, nine-to-five way?"

5. How does the author choose to resolve Harrah's "severe sleep disorder" in "Night and Day You Are the One?"

6. What kind of a person is Tom, the protagonist in "Rope Bridge?" At one point, Lucy says that love is "the most ephemeral thing in the world. In the end, it diminishes into just another responsibility." How do the events in "Rope Bridge" support, refute, or qualify her lament?

7. For "No Grace on the Road," discuss the nature and complexities of the narrator's ambivalence regarding his heritage, his American wife, and the effects that French colonialism appear to have had on his native culture. Does the narrator have a true home? Consider how the narrator juxtaposes two explanations for why monsoons occur—one a detached Western account grounded in science, the other an ancient Eastern myth full of wonder and allegory. Why does the author do this?

8. Contrast the significance and potential after-effects of the sex act that occurs at the climax of "Rope Bridge" with the sex act at the conclusion of "No Grace on the Road."

9. In "Suit," why do you suppose the author chooses to reveal so slowly and deliberately the whole situation that has led up to the characters' shopping expedition? Discuss the techniques Kalfus uses in doing this. Have you ever read any similarly structured stories?

10. In "A Line Is a Series of Points," how does the author's economy of language serve this story's tone and theme? Why has the author chosen not to tell us the nationality of the refugees?

11. What is the meaning of *home* in this collection? Compare the protagonist in "A Line Is a Series of Points" with those in "Among the Bulgarians" and "No Grace on the Road."

12. The fourteen stories in *Thirst* comprise a wide range of styles, emotions, and geographies. What themes does it consider? When you read it, what surprised you the most? Can you compare Kalfus to other writers? Whom? Which stories do you think are the most effective? Why?

## AUTHOR QUESTIONS

**Q. Each story in *Thirst* is stylistically distinct. How do you set out creating the language or the voice in which you tell your stories?**

A. In some of these stories, like "The Joy and Melancholy Baseball Trivia Quiz," the narrative strategy came to me before the story itself; for example, I wanted to write a short story in the form of a trivia quiz. The narrative style *is* the story, and that's true to some extent for even more conventionally told narratives. Many writers have discovered that how you tell a story—its voice and point of view—determines its effect much more than the plot does.

**Q. Tell us about your travels, where you've lived, and how these experiences might have influenced your writing.**

A. I've been lucky to live abroad a bit, in Paris, Dublin, Belgrade and Moscow, and have done some traveling, and all that finds itself in what I write but always a bit refracted. Years ago I worked as a babysitter in Paris, between stints as an investment banker and brain surgeon. I recall visiting a museum like the one described in "Le Jardin de la Sexualité," but, alas, have never been able to find it again.

**Q. Your stories are full of magic, absurdity, innovative structure, darkness, and major leaps of imagination. Are you going to stick to the short story form, or can we look forward to a novel?**

A. The short story form invites playfulness; the novel naturally allows for more character depth and complication. My new book, "PU-239 and Other Russian Fantasies," includes several longer stories and a short novel, and I hope maintains that element of play. I'm working on a full length novel now.

Breinigsville, PA USA
12 November 2009
227485BV00002B/78/A